**"If you continue to flirt
with other men, wife,"
he whispered,**

"I shall take it as a signal that you are in need of my attentions. Tonight will be repeated as often as you make a spectacle of yourself."

"What—what are you saying? Are you joking?"

"No. Merely telling you to conduct yourself with an eye to counting the cost of your lavishly endowed 'melting glances.'"

Eleanor went cold with fury. Her breath seemed to leave her body. "You don't know what you've done, Geoffrey. You'll never have me again. I loathe you. You've taken whatever love may have been growing between us and destroyed it more completely than if you had destroyed me."

Her body that had so recently been flushed with love now felt encased in the same ice that seemed to fill her heart...

Dear Reader:

As the months go by, we continue to receive word from you that SECOND CHANCE AT LOVE romances are providing you with the kind of romantic entertainment you're looking for. In your letters you've voiced enthusiastic support for SECOND CHANCE AT LOVE, you've shared your thoughts on how personally meaningful the books are, and you've suggested ideas and changes for future books. Although we can't always reply to your letters as quickly as we'd like, please be assured that we appreciate your comments. Your thoughts are all-important to us!

We're glad many of you have come to associate SECOND CHANCE AT LOVE books with our butterfly trademark. We think the butterfly is a perfect symbol of the reaffirmation of life and thrilling new love that SECOND CHANCE AT LOVE heroines and heroes find together in each story. We hope you keep asking for the "butterfly books," and that, when you buy one—whether by a favorite author or a talented new writer—you're sure of a good read. You can trust all SECOND CHANCE AT LOVE books to live up to the high standards of romantic fiction you've come to expect.

So happy reading, and keep your letters coming!

With warm wishes,

Ellen Edwards

Ellen Edwards
SECOND CHANCE AT LOVE
The Berkley/Jove Publishing Group
200 Madison Avenue
New York, NY 10016

CS

Second Chance at Love

REGENCY

THE FORGOTTEN BRIDE
LILLIAN MARSH

A
SECOND CHANCE AT LOVE
BOOK

THE FORGOTTEN BRIDE

First edition published January 1983

First printing

"Second Chance at Love" and the butterfly emblem are trademarks belonging to Jove Publications, Inc.

Printed in the United States of America

Second Chance at Love books are published by
The Berkley/Jove Publishing Group
200 Madison Avenue, New York, NY 10016

TO MY PARENTS

PROLOGUE

THE SOFT APRIL breeze moved gently through the newly budded blossoms of the lilacs and hedge roses that edged the narrow lane. The pale green of early leaves covered the branches of trees that grew here and there in the fields, but their beauty made no impression on the solitary driver seated behind a matched pair of bay geldings that drew a dashing black curricle along the country road.

The reins of the equipage were held loosely by the auburn-haired, gray-eyed young man dressed in a dashing, many-caped driving coat. A flat-topped beaver was tilted over one eyebrow, giving him an air of bravado that was belied by the misery reflected in his eyes. Though handsome, his face was still soft with youth, not yet having been shaped by the experiences of life. Occasionally he drew a silver flask from the pocket of his coat and raised it to his lips, drinking deeply from its contents.

"Oh, Alvinia, how could you have betrayed our love . . . for a title and a mound of shekels?" he demanded of the air around him. "How could you have thrown away our love? But I'll show you . . . I'll show you! I'll . . . I'll marry the first girl I find!" He interrupted his soliloquy with another pull at the flask of brandy, then contemplated his situation morosely.

Geoffrey de Maine had just suffered his first disappointment in love. At twenty-four, he faced it with all the intensity of feeling of which youth is capable. A younger son of a noble family, he had been secretly betrothed to Alvinia Bryce and had convinced the young woman to elope with him because of her parents' objections to the match. Geoffrey was the second son of an earl and, although he had a sufficient competence, he was not as attractive to the elder Bryces as a titled nobleman of greater wealth.

Geoffrey had met Alvinia while enjoying his first season in London. A series of illnesses during his late teens had delayed his introduction to the *ton* and his cultivation of the sophistication that might normally be his at twenty-four.

He had been introduced to Alvinia at Almack's and had immediately been smitten by her tight golden ringlets and slumbrous blue eyes. At twenty, she was years older in experience than the naïve young man four years her senior. It pleased her to keep him dangling, and when he pleaded with her to elope with him, she agreed, thinking it delicious that she should add his scalp to her rapidly growing collection of eligible males. Without weighing the damage it might do to his ego to be jilted, she had promised to marry him as soon as he was able to procure a special license, knowing that she would never do such a thing. He had hastened to her side, license in hand, triumphant in the thought that they would soon be wed. Upon his arrival at her home, he had found that, in the two weeks since the plans had been made, she had become the wife of Baron Edward Coddington, a wealthy elderly peer.

When he had learned that the woman he thought of as the love of his life was now beyond his reach, Geoffrey had taken himself to the nearest tavern. He had spent three days drowning his sorrows and finally, to his amazement, had become bored as well as thoroughly ill. He did not usually become inebriated in answer to life's disappointments, but having read the poets, he had learned that one had a choice between suicide or drink as an answer to a broken heart. He had chosen the latter as being the less final solution. Not that he spent much time debating the matter with himself. It was an unconscious decision that arose from his normally carefree disposition. But young men suffer intensely and must, if needs be, assuage the suffering by extreme means. That Geoffrey chose drowning in brandy instead of drowning in the sea was a credit to his native good sense, lost though it might be for the moment.

Once the young man had finished with the measures he had chosen to relieve the pain of his loss, he had bathed, dined and slept, awakening that morning with a firm decision to return to the bosom of his family. Not yet able to face life without a modicum of fortification, he had filled his flask with the landlord's best and had imbibed freely en route. He was no more than two sheets to the wind because he held his liquor well, but he had consumed enough to surround events with a slight haze.

As the conveyance moved along the way, the lane became part of a larger road. Geoffrey kept carefully to the side, aware that his perceptions were a shade under par. In the distance he could see a large brick building set back from the road and surrounded by a wall that enclosed the posting yard of the busy hostelry. The London Mail was just leaving, the postilion having just sounded a loud blast on the yard of tin he carried to warn other vehicles out of the way.

The rejected suitor, wishing to replenish his supply of spiritous liquor, guided his team between the high wrought-iron gates that stood wide open in welcome to weary travelers arriving at the inn. He tossed the reins to a waiting ostler with orders to feed and water the horses, admonishing the servant not to put them up for the night.

The ground seemed to be a trifle unsteady beneath his feet, but by paying attention to the placement of his steps, the young man proceeded to enter the open door awaiting him. The hospitable host made much of his arrival, assuring him that he would find the table to his satisfaction and privacy guaranteed if he would but condescend to enter the private parlor just readied for his appearance. Geoffrey graciously allowed the innkeeper to conduct him to the spacious apartment that had been set aside for the more affluent guests of the place. A fire flickered warmly, taking the chill from the room and beckoning the tired traveler to its comfort. A lounge chair was set at an appropriate distance from the hearth with a small dining table nearby.

"If . . . if you wo-ould p-p-please bring me s-s-some brandy?" The care with which he enunciated his words hid the state of Geoffrey's inebriation. "F-f-food also."

Quickly mine host called upon his minions to fill his guest's needs. With a giggle, the servant girls prepared a heavy tray of food and half-ran through the hallway with it. In their hurry, they missed seeing the figure hovering on the staircase, wrapped closely in a dark cloak and carrying a carpet bag from which escaped bits and pieces of lace and muslin.

From within the protection of a large hood that topped the gray wool cape, a pair of frightened hazel eyes watched the door through which the two maids had disappeared. Before more than a few moments passed, the two ran from the room, giggling outrageously and cautioning the guest to mind his manners.

The slightly built young woman waited impatiently until there was nothing more alarming to be heard than the low rumble of voices from the public room and the clatter of pots, pans, and dishes from the kitchens to the rear of the building. Tentatively, she lowered a foot to the next step, hesitating as though afraid it would break beneath her weight. A creak of a door from above and then a sound like a groan brought a look of frantic fear to the wide eyes. Quickly, as a hare fleeing in the forest, she ran down the remaining steps and whirled into the room where Geoffrey was enjoying his meal. Panic-stricken, she leaned her body against the door, as though her frail weight would bar an intruder from entering.

"J-j-just what d-d-do you think you're d-d-doing here, my g-g-girl?" The young man was still suffering from the results of his overindulgence.

"Oh, sir, I beg you, please let me stay for a moment. I am in the most dire trouble." The girl turned to Geoffrey, her hood slipping back from her hair to reveal a sweetly curved cheek, limpid greenish-gold eyes, and a soft mouth above a firm chin. The whole was capped by a cloud of dark hair caught up in a Psyche knot that was showing a decided tendency to slip from its place.

Geoffrey, his mind somewhat rattled, heard the fear in the gentle voice but, still wary of females owing to his recent heartbreak, he responded with a decidedly suspicious grunt.

"I know this is all very unusual, but I am truly in need. Well . . . at least I need someone who will help me to escape my present situation." The young woman moved to the table and pulled a chair away from it to seat herself, showing a poise that was at odds with her frightened manner when she had first entered the room. "Oh, this food looks wonderful. Do you mind if I help myself? I haven't been fed since early this morning, and that was just a roll and some water. Ummm. I'll have a bit of the beef and perhaps a smidgen of the ham and oh, I must taste the pudding and . . ." The fear that had been so apparent had abated as it was replaced with delight at the sumptuous table set for the young man.

"Thought you was in t-t-trouble. . . . Never knew a w-w-woman to eat when she was in t-t-trouble."

"Oh, I *am* in trouble. Great trouble. But I never knew it to help if one had to starve to death, did you? I can eat and tell you my story at the same time, and then you can come up with a plan to save me." The young woman

placed herself very matter-of-factly in Geoffrey's un-
willing hands.

Before he could comment upon the situation, she introduced herself as Eleanor Glyndon, an orphan and ward
of Gilbert Ronsville, friend and gambling companion of
her deceased father, who had been an extremely poor
judge of character. Mr. Ronsville, who was a thoroughgoing knave, had accepted Eleanor as his ward, hoping
to enjoy her young charms in lieu of the capital needed
to support her.

"He brought me to this inn to make me his mistress,
but I won't allow that. I'd sooner run off with the gypsies."
A flush of outrage colored the delicate porcelain skin.
"If you could please take me with you when you leave
here..."

"Where's the s-s-scoundrel now? I should think he'd
be right after you." Geoffrey had noticed the absence of
clamor following his companion's entrance into the parlor.

"Well I... When he..." Dark lashes fluttered down,
hiding the woman's glowing eyes. "I hit him with the
candlestick when he slobbered his nasty wet kisses all
over my face!"

Slightly bloodshot gray eyes stared incredulously at
the demurely bowed head across the table. "You hit him
with the candlestick? Did you kill him?"

"Oh, no... I wouldn't do that no matter how horrid
he is. He's more like asleep... for a good while I hope."
Shapely hands deftly cut a morsel of sirloin of beef and
raised it delicately to the pink lips. "Now, what do you
suggest we do?"

"Out of curiosity, h-h-how old are you?" Geoffrey
asked.

"I shall be eighteen on my next birthday, which really
should be old enough to look after myself, but isn't by
law." The sangfroid with which Eleanor had seemed to
imbue her story disappeared from her manner, and the

fear that really drove her was once more apparent in her face. "Truly, I should be so grateful if you would help me. I'm sure I could find work as a governess or something once I got away from that despicable man." A tear trembled on her long eyelashes.

Geoffrey poured himself another glass of robust claret, the finest from mine host's cellars. His broad forehead wrinkled as he thought about the problem before him. Slowly the wrinkles disappeared as a sardonic grin twisted his lips. He lifted his eyes to Eleanor's, his once-open smile showing an unexpected jump into maturity. The naïve young man was no longer the unknowing green youngster who had arrived in London barely four months ago.

"I've got the answer, my girl. I'll marry you and that will make *me* your guardian. Then you'll not have to worry about Ronsville bothering you any more."

"Don't be foolish—how can you marry me? I don't even know your name!" Eleanor continued to partake of the food as though she were not startled by Geoffrey's pronouncement.

With a slight list to the left, Geoffrey rose to his feet and bowed low, clutching the table to prevent his falling on the floor.

"May I present myself to you, madam? Geoffrey de Maine at your service." His proper introduction ended in a small hiccup.

"I am pleased to make your acquaintance, sir." Eleanor stood and curtsied to just the proper depth upon meeting someone of her own rank. "Please be seated."

"Thank you, Miss Glyndon." Carefully, he found the edge of the chair and backed onto it. "Now, to resume our plans. I happen to have with me a special license, so there'll be no problem as long as we can find a parson. You, Miss Glyndon, must watch the hall and, as soon as it's clear, make for my curricle—it's the black one with the matched bays—and get into it. I shall pay the landlord and be with you in a trice, and then we'll head back to London. I think it will be easiest to find a willing minister nearer there—and harder for your guardian to find you. Once we're married, I'll take you home to my mother, or you can go your own way, whichever you prefer."

"Oh, but... to marry me. How do we know that we'd suit? I'm not at all sure I wish to marry." Worried eyes sought reassurance from the young man.

"Don't concern yourself about it. I give you my oath I'll protect you and give you a home. I must tell you you'll never have my heart; it's been broken in two by a most unfeeling girl." Geoffrey paused a moment to contemplate his betrayed sensibilities. "But eventually I should have to marry in any case, if only to please my parents, so it might as well be you. You look like a nice enough little thing, and, if my marrying you will help in your time of trouble, why then, so be it. Now watch the hallway and no more talk, or I'll begin to think you'd rather stay with your guardian."

Eleanor cast a wondering gaze at her heroic rescuer. That he was suffering from pangs of a lost love was quite evident to her discerning eye, but that he should be so gracious as to offer marriage to save her from her guardian placed him on another level entirely. He had suddenly become surrounded by a shining aura such as she had imagined enveloped Sir Galahad or Sir Launcelot when she had read about them in Malory's *Morte d'Arthur*.

Afraid that he might change his mind before they were away from the inn, Eleanor slipped from the room and out to the posting yard, where she quickly found the described carriage. She looked around to make sure she was unobserved, climbed onto the front seat, then ducked beneath it, covering herself with the thick fur robe in an attempt to hide from prying eyes.

It seemed an eternity before she felt the curricle dip in response to the weight of Geoffrey's body as he lifted

himself up and took possession of the driving seat. She
heard the slide of the whip handle against the holding
socket as he removed it from its place, then the *swish* of
the lash as he flicked it against the backs of the horses
and the slap of the reins against their bodies. Very slowly
the rig began to move in response to the clip-clop of the
horses' hooves. The girl could barely breathe, so great
was her anxiety that her guardian might recover consciousness and discover her absence before she was safely
away. Now that she was finally making her escape, she
could wonder at her insouciant behavior when she had
sat at Geoffrey's table, eating his dinner. How could she
have paid so little heed to her situation? Perhaps even
then she had felt the safety that Mr. de Maine's company
offered her. Despite his slow and somewhat slurred
speech, he seemed to know what he was about.

When Geoffrey at last called to her to come out from
under the rug, Eleanor was more than ready to join him.
As she slid onto the seat, she turned her head to take a
long look back at the way they had traveled, but in the
fifteen minutes or so since they had left the inn, they had
come far enough so that the building was no longer in
view.

"I believe that there will be no dogs on your track this
day, Miss Glyndon. I made sure that the innkeeper thinks
that I am bent on traveling to Reading. In reality, we
shall head toward Godalming. We're sure to find a parson
somewhere between there and Dorking." The young man
glanced at his companion, noting that her dark hair had
become disheveled and her nose covered with dust during
her short sojourn under the fur. "We'll stop shortly so
that you can straighten yourself. You don't quite have
the look of a bride, I'm afraid. Can you act the role, do
you think?" Mr. de Maine took an encouraging nip from
his ever-present flask.

"Are you in pain, Mr. de Maine?" The girl fixed a
questioning look upon Geoffrey. "My father used to carry

his medicine about in just such a silver bottle as that. Oh, I do beg your pardon. I shall tidy my hair and put on a bonnet. I have one here in my satchel. It might be a tiny bit crushed, but the ribands are the prettiest color. Cherry red." She reached for the bag and began to undo the fastening. "Mrs. Mortimer, the vicar's wife, gave it to me for a going-away present. It was an old bonnet of Lady Hambrough's, but Mrs. Mortimer put the new ribands on it so that it would look more suitable for someone my age because Mrs. Hambrough is rather elderly, and what is suitable for her is . . ." Abruptly the high, breathy voice came to a halt as tears, held so tightly controlled for so long, spilled down the velvety cheeks. "Oh, I do so beg your pardon, sir . . . I . . . I . . ."

"So, so . . ." soothed Geoffrey, taking the quivering girl in his arms. "You look just like my youngest sister when she has an attack of the dismals and must cry it all out." He shifted the reins gently before they could become entangled around Eleanor's body. "Just cry away until you feel better." He edged himself closer to his passenger, pulling her against his body as he offered her the comfort of his person. Her crying gradually became sobs that softened and slowed until only an occasional hiccup echoed in the still afternoon air.

As the tears ended, Eleanor became aware of Geoffrey's arms and the intimate association of their bodies on the carriage seat. Reluctantly, not wishing to leave the comforting strength of her about-to-be bridegroom, she began to pull away from him, only to find herself restrained by that same strength.

"Please don't move. I don't mind you sitting so close, and if we want to make time, I should hold onto you so you don't get bounced around so much." Secretly enjoying the responses Eleanor's soft body was invoking in him, Geoffrey found excuses for continuing to hold her.

Like two babes in the wood, the young couple took comfort in each other's warmth, and the distance between

Aldershot and Godalming was soon covered.

As luck would have it, they soon found themselves in front of a small, ivy-covered church on the outskirts of the village. A short distance beyond the church was the vicar's residence. The flower-filled garden and the sound of children laughing made them believe that they might have found someone who would help them in their need.

Although the minister professed reluctance to perform a wedding ceremony between such young people without the presence of a parent, his wife, who was most romantically inclined, convinced him that the special license to wed was enough to sanction the marriage. She smiled most agreeably at Eleanor as she handed her a bouquet of posies that she had gathered. "Every bride should have flowers on her wedding day, my dear, so do carry these so that you will have a keepsake to put away to show your children."

A passing shepherd was called upon to give the bride away, and the wedding ring was the small signet that Geoffrey wore on the little finger of his left hand. When the vicar called for any who objected to this marriage, Eleanor held her breath, dreading that her guardian might have discovered her whereabouts. Finally, the words "I now pronounce you man and wife," were heard and a burst of congratulations rose from the heretofore-silent shepherd and the minister's smiling wife.

A sip of wine and some freshly baked cake were pressed upon the newlyweds in honor of the occasion, but as quickly as politeness allowed, Geoffrey drew Eleanor away from the church. Once more the two were on their way.

It seemed to the bride that, once they were again on the road, her new husband resorted with greater frequency to his silver flask. Although his posture showed no effect of the "medicine," his words became a bit more indistinct. The sun was already setting when Geoffrey decided that the small hostelry they were approaching would be an appropriate place to spend the night.

"Here y'are then, sir and mistress," the short, fat innkeeper addressed them. "This is the only room left, and it'll do you just fine, I'm sure."

"But, I thought... that is..." Eleanor was too embarrassed to express the hope that they were to have had separate rooms.

"This is excellent, landlord. We shall signal you when we are ready to sup." Geoffrey's words ignored Eleanor's attempt to establish a platonic relationship between them. "My wife and I are quite tired from our day's traveling and would take our rest before we dine."

"Certainly, sir, most certainly." Bowing and scraping, the host took himself off.

"You... we... ah, we didn't speak of our actually being husband and wife, Mr. de Maine." Eleanor's voice was not much above a whisper.

"But what would be more natural, Mrs. de Maine, than for us to comfort one another?" Geoffrey moved to take the young woman in his arms. "After all, I have bleshed... breshed... b-les-sed you with my name, so I see no problemsh." He bent his head to take possession of a pair of sweet pink lips before they could utter a denial to his wishes.

Suddenly, to the befuddled young man, his marital rights became the most important issue to be faced. He became blinded to the chastity of his new wife and saw in her the fulfillment of the need he had felt all during his courtship of Alvinia. True, he had taken himself a lady of the night once or twice, but his romantic heart had not been satisfied. His innate fastidiousness found no attraction in such random coupling.

Here before him was a woman he had rights to— clean, smelling of spice and flowers, warm and rounded. What better way to assuage his heartbreak than in his wife's sweet flesh. Without recognizing her instinctive withdrawal as the normal fear of a virginal maiden, he pressed his kisses on her mouth, holding her tightly in the circle of his arms. He was intoxicated enough to unleash the bonds of civil behavior, but not enough to douse the fires of his easily ignited passion. He ignored Eleanor's fluttering hands that were trying to push away from him.

"Come, sweet one, let us play at being husband and wife. 'Tis a most wondrous game and you shall enjoy it, I promise." His lips pursued the line of her chin to her earlobe, paused to nibble at it, then stopped a while at the pulse that beat so erratically at the base of her neck. While he was busy at that pursuit, his hand moved from her waist, approaching and then capturing the softly rounded globe of her breast, stroking it to a stiffened response that shocked Eleanor at the same time that it caused a dartlike flame to glow in her loins.

"Oh, no . . . you mustn't . . . this wasn't . . ." The girl murmured objections helplessly, her mind trying to control the physical awareness that had been awakened by Geoffrey's enticing kisses and urgent caresses. How amazing that she felt so different in Geoffrey's arms than she had felt in Ronsville's.

"Here, sweet wife, let me help you disrobe . . . 'tis a most gratifying concurrence that we both seek the same release for our disappointments." His fingers unbuttoned the dimity bodice diligently, sliding it from her shoulders as he held her immmobile with a deep kiss. Then he unloosed the strings of her skirt and petticoat, lifting her bodily out of them as they fell to the floor. He lifted her in his arms and carried her to the bed, not releasing her lips from his. "Now, sweetling, help me from my clothes as I have helped you."

Frightened, aroused, even intrigued in a small way by what was happening to her, Eleanor tentatively offered a minor amount of aid. Geoffrey, too excited by the situation and too inexperienced in the art of love to teach his bride the game, hastened to bed his bride and continued what was in essence the ravishment of an innocent girl. She felt his hard body thrust against the softness of hers, then a sharp pain followed by a discomfort that continued for several moments until her husband fell away from her to rest supine by her side. She felt a consuming sadness that her hero was unworthy of his name, and a disappointment that their marriage was not as she had thought.

Tears fell from the girl's eyes. Her introduction to womanhood had held none of the romance that she had pictured when she had read of the joys of love. It would seem that, except for the marriage lines that had been given into her hand earlier that day, her spouse had used her no differently than her guardian would have had she not run away. At least she was protected by that piece of paper. Geoffrey said he would take her to his home, wherever that might be... and perhaps he would soon tire of this activity and seek his pleasures elsewhere.

Eleanor fell asleep, only to be awakened some time later by the importunities of her bridegroom. This time he had slept off some of the effects of his drinking and was a more thoughtful lover. To Eleanor's surprise, she found her body responding to the caresses of his hands and mouth. When he took her, she was almost ready to enjoy the sensations that filled her.

Once more before dawn her lover approached, this time bringing her to that sublime awareness that is the result of a mutual expression of the passions of the flesh. Her sighs and cries joined his as they reached the peak of their endeavor at the same moment. But then her newly found bliss was destroyed when his voice cried out "Alvinia" as his body shuddered in release.

At the hour after dawn Geoffrey de Maine awakened clear-eyed and clear-headed. He found himself sharing a bed with a dark-haired female in an unclothed condition, who was fast asleep. Her face was nestled into the pillow, preventing him from viewing it clearly. His situation led him to the conclusion that at some point the previous day he had found himself a Cyprian with whom he had drowned his sorrows and found his joys.

He dressed himself, quietly, not wishing to awaken the girl, who no doubt would ask for a prolonged farewell. He reached into his pocket and removed his well-laden purse. He carefully counted out a few guineas, adding several more for the guilt he felt at leaving her without a good-bye, and placed them on the bureau. With a hasty glance around the room to see whether he had overlooked anything, he removed himself from the chamber and out of the inn.

Returned sobriety had brought a loss of memory of the preceding twenty-four hours. He forgot the girl he had married, the promises he had made her, and the hopes she had expressed.

Geoffrey de Maine was on his way home to Cornwall.

CHAPTER ONE

THE CRACKLE OF the fire and the occasional slide of paper against paper were the only sounds in the exquisitely paneled library. The large room was furnished with handsome tapestry-covered couches and chairs upholstered in the French manner. Polished wood tables, some three hundred years old, stood next to the various chairs, holding many-branched candelabra and bibelots collected from around the world. An unusual Chinese *sang de boeuf* vase was next to an early Byzantine chalice. A delicate cloisonné miniature of sixteenth century Venetian origin stood side by side with a bowl recently executed by Josiah Wedgwood.

Seated at the large Louis Quinze desk was a coldly handsome man whose head was bent over the long curl of paper that was crossed and recrossed with an almost illegible handwriting. Geoffrey de Maine, Earl of Hellistone, was trying to decipher a letter written by his sister, Madeline, who was at present visiting her godmother in Bath. The letter seemed to be a list of complaints. Her wardrobe was inadequate, the weather was cold, the entertainments were too lofty for a young woman. But—hosannahs!—she had been described as an original, an incomparable, and a gem of the first water.

Annoyed with his sister's shallow delights, the earl tossed the letter to the desk top and pushed himself away from the massive piece of furniture. He walked over to one of the windows that looked out onto the renowned gardens of Pentalwyn Hall, which were not yet abloom in this late winter season. Beyond the gardens he could see the rolling landscape that stretched to the rocky coast of Cornwall.

The cold, wintry light suited his mood as he contemplated the scene before him. Years before, he had taken delight in his home, but since his return from Waterloo and his succession to the title after the unexpected demise of both his father and his elder brother in a boating accident, Geoffrey de Maine could no longer find the easy enjoyment in the simple pleasures that had once made him happy. He wondered if he were doing the right thing in marrying Alvinia, Lady Coddington, now that she was the widow of Sir Edward. She had destroyed his youth when she had married the old man, but had expressed her distress at being forced into marriage with a man so much older than herself. He chose to believe her sentiments; at least she would be a suitable partner and would expect nothing more than the position his fortune and title would provide. Love was no longer mentioned between them, at least not on his part. Alvinia chose to pretend an abiding passion when they were alone.

A knock at the door disturbed his reverie.

"Come!" he commanded, turning to see who it was.

"My Lord." Chiswick, butler for as long as the earl could remember, entered the chamber. "A lady, my lord, has requested an audience with you. I told her..." Chiswick seemed to have been unsettled by his meeting with the "lady."

"Well, man, get on with it, who is she?" The earl's aquiline features no longer reflected any of the softness that had been there in his younger years.

"She didn't say, my lord. She just insisted that she must see you most urgently. I tried to tell her that you see no one without an appointment, but she wouldn't leave. She sat herself down in the second parlor and said she would wait until you agreed to an appointment." The elderly servant shook his head. "But she *is* a lady, my lord, there's no doubt on that score. She came in a small private coach, and I caught a glimpse of two other persons still in the carriage."

A dark eyebrow lifted over a cool gray eye. "Very well, Chiswick, if you call her a lady, then I must surely agree to see her. Bring her in." The earl turned his back on his servant to study the landscape once more.

Through the now-open door the earl could hear the rustle of silk and padding of footsteps as his visitor, accompanied by the butler, walked toward the library. There was a lack of haste in the pacing of the visitor's walk and even an insolence, if the occasional pauses as though to study one of the paintings that hung on the walls of the hallway were any indication.

Annoyed at the presumption of his unknown guest, de Maine moved to his desk, wondering about this person who had demanded an interview.

His attitude towards women being what it was, he was unprepared for his reaction to the lady who appeared in the doorway to the library. She was not much above medium height, but she carried herself with the air of a princess. Her clear white complexion seemed to him to be like translucent porcelain overlaid with a hint of roses. Her eyes, which were shadowed by long lashes, were golden and touched by a flash of green. Her face was oval, divided into portions by gracefully arched eyebrows, a straight nose, and lips that might have hinted at a sensuousness of nature were they not held together so tightly.

The earl felt a *frisson* of memory touch him, almost as though he had seen the woman at some other time, but he shrugged his shoulders in rejection of the thought and allowed a look of indolent hauteur to rove over the curves of her body, resting at last on her beautiful face.

She was dressed in the height of fashion. A deep rose-colored pelisse adorned with fur around the neck and at the hem was buttoned over a dress of pale pink challis. Gray gloves of hand-worked kid covered her hands and matched the gray half-boots on her feet. A small brimmed hat decorated with a saucy curled plume tilted daringly over one eye, revealing the soft curls of her dark hair.

Once through the doorway, she paused at the edge of the Persian carpet, studying him, waiting for his response. Her heart was beating with such force that she felt it rising into her throat, and she couldn't have uttered a word in that moment had her life depended upon it. She had thought of him constantly in the months after their marriage, wondering why he had left her without a word after having claimed his rights as her husband on their wedding night. He had taught her what passion was and had seemed pleased with her response. But when she had awakened, expecting to feel once more his warm arms and the taut, lean strength of his body, he had been gone, a pile of golden guineas the only sign that he had ever been there. If it had not been for the marriage certificate in her reticule, she would have doubted her own memory.

She gazed at his face, once so beloved in her thoughts, now unfamiliar to her sight. There was no remnant of the young man she had married. What had been an unformed, sweetly handsome face was now cold and autocratic. He held himself stiffly upright, hand on hip, challenging her right to be in this place. His gray eyes were icy and filled with an unexpected animosity, as though her appearance displeased him. She had known that this meeting would be difficult, but she had not expected to be met with enmity and the blank lack of recognition.

She bowed her head in greeting as she said, "My lord."

"Madam," he acknowledged her presence. "You wished to see me. To what purpose?"

"Do you not offer the hospitality of a seat to a visitor, my lord?" With supreme effort she hid her shock at his cold regard.

Her tranquil voice and direct attack startled him. The Earl of Hellistone looked to no one to remind him of his manners.

"If you will, madam." He gestured to a small fauteuil, betraying his anger at her insolence in the sharpness of his voice. "What is this urgent matter that has brought you into my home, madam? Who are you and why are you here?"

Ignoring his question, Eleanor took the seat offered her. She stripped off her gloves and arranged them on her lap, keeping a tight rein on her feelings, hoping that the tremor that swept through her would not be apparent to him.

"I believe you placed an announcement in the *London Times,* my lord, stating that you have become betrothed to the Lady Alvinia Coddington?"

Geoffrey's eyebrows arched in response to the inquiry. "What has that to do with your visit here?"

"Is Lady Coddington the same lady who . . . jilted . . . you some eight years ago, my lord?" Eleanor's voice remained quiet, almost offhand, as she spoke.

"Madam, you will answer me at once!" His temper began to flare. "What is your business here? What kind of insinuations are you making?"

"Regretfully, my lord, I have come to tell you that you will have to retract your offer of marriage to Lady Coddington." Eleanor paused as though to gauge the impact of her next words. "I have come to tell you that you will be committing bigamy should you marry *anyone.* You are already married!"

Gray eyes opened wide in amazement; then a chill

laugh rang out. "You most certainly are an original, madam. You arrive at my home unknown and uninvited, forbear to tell me your name, but caution me that I am married. What's your game? Is this some scheme by which you hope to gain some vast sum of money from me?"

Eleanor maintained her calm demeanor, not yet understanding fully why her husband should deny his wedded state. "I have no need for your money, sir, and my name, which should have been known to you for these past eight years, is Eleanor de Maine, now Countess Hellistone."

"You are mad, madam." Geoffrey leaned against the desk, looking like a tiger ready to spring on its prey. "What farrago of nonsense is this? I have never been married, and certainly not to you." His eyes roamed over her face and body, mentally undressing her as though she were merchandise to be examined for his purchase. "Bed you I might, but wed you... I think not. Now, enough of this. There is no way you can inveigle me to change my plans, so you might as well take yourself off, madam, before I send for the magistrate."

As the earl spoke, Eleanor reached into her reticule and withdrew a folded paper and a small piece of jewelry. Her eyes ablaze, she handed them to him. "I think you should look at our marriage lines, my lord, and that you will also recognize this ring." She sat still, waiting for the tall auburn-haired man to walk to her side.

He accepted the ring silently, his face paling at the sight of the small signet that his mother had given him on his eighteenth birthday. He had missed it years ago and had always wondered what had become of it. He slipped it onto his little finger before glancing at the slightly worn parchment. He read the lines that attested to the fact that Eleanor Glyndon had become the wife of Geoffrey de Maine on the seventeenth day of April in the year of our Lord 1812 in the village of Godalming,

Hampshire, joined that day by the Reverend Arthur C. Badger, D.D.

"This is impossible. I have no recollection of the event." The earl rubbed the back of his neck as though to stimulate his memory. "How did this come about? I don't recall ever having met you before."

"You were on your way to your home when we met at an inn just outside Aldershot, my lord. I was about to be ravished by my guardian, but I . . . laid him low with a candlestick and ran from his 'protection.' You were dining in the private parlor, and when I prevailed upon you to help me, you informed me that we could be wed because you had an unused special license in your pocket. You told me that you planned on an elopement with Alvinia Bryce, but that she had married a wealthy, titled old man instead, and you were determined to make use of the license. You were also imbibing very heavily from a silver flask as well as from the stores of the inn, but I was too inexperienced to realize you must have been quite inebriated.

"In any case, we left the inn and found the Reverend Mr. Badger, who performed the ceremony. You then took me to another hostelry, where you introduced me to the . . . charms . . . of wedded bliss. When I awoke in the morning, you had gone, leaving me an amount of money on the bureau. I never knew why you had taken that action, sir, after you had promised to love, honor, and cherish me. Eventually I learned to cope with the disappearance of my husband."

"Why did you not make yourself known to me years ago? Surely it would have been to your benefit."

"You forget, my lord, that you never gave me your direction. I had met you in Hampshire and knew you as Geoffrey de Maine. When I inquired, I learned that there were no de Maines within fifty miles of where we met. I was very young, very innocent, and very distraught. I had no sponsor to help me and managed to survive the first few weeks only by living in a most humble way, stretching the guineas you left me so that they would last as long as possible. I had used them all and was wandering down a lane near Petersfield when I fainted. To my everlasting good fortune, I was found by a Miss Shappley, a recluse who lived in the area. She was a retired actress who, perhaps because of her own experiences in the world, took me in and cared for me until her death two years ago. Since then I have lived quietly with Phillip and Mrs. Ogden, who was Miss Shappley's attendant and is now my companion. When I saw your announcement in the *Times,* I knew that I must come forward to prevent your committing so terrible an injustice."

"You have the effrontery to tell me you have lived all these years with this man Phillip and now wish to be recognized as my wife?" The Arctic could have been no colder than the earl's voice.

"I must ask your indulgence for a moment, sir." Eleanor stood and walked quickly to the door. "I would like you to meet Phillip."

The earl's face flushed with wrath. The shock of meeting a wife he had never known he had, the thought of the brangle that would follow his announcement that he would no longer be able to honor his betrothal, and the easy manner in which the woman had responded to his anger combined to hold him motionless for the few moments that passed before Eleanor returned to the library.

She walked into the room followed by a tall, imposing woman dressed in the sober garments that announced her as a companion to the lady. Holding the countess by the hand was a boy, carrot-headed and open-faced, but of a curious dignity for one so young.

"My lord, I make you acquainted with Phillip de Maine. Phillip, make your bow to your father." Eleanor drew the boy forward to face the man who was held motionless by the enormity of what he had just heard.

The child straightened and stood with his hands by his side, feet together. He ducked his head in a short, almost regal gesture, acknowledging Geoffrey with a "sir" as he did so.

Except for his coloring, the boy looked like his mother. But his eyes were the de Maine eyes, that clear lucid gray with the dark ring around the outer edge of the iris, and with deep-set eyelids that were not yet pronounced in such a youngster but were indicated by the shape. There was no denying the fact that the child carried de Maine blood.

Father and son studied each other, the younger with the curious innocence of youth, the older with the incredible knowledge that he was responsible for the birth of a human being of whom he had been totally unaware until this moment. At last Geoffrey took a deep breath. For the time being he must accept the situation. The papers seemed to be in order. Until he could speak to his solicitor and his man of business, he would perforce allow the woman to remain in his home.

Eleanor stood quietly, watching her husband. He was an undeciphered quantity to her. She had once known him for less than twenty-four hours, and eight years had passed since then. She was concerned only that her son should be acknowledged by his father. With that recognition would come a secure future for Phillip. Money was not the reason: Miss Shappley had left her fortune to the forgotten bride. Instead, Eleanor had come to Pentalwyn Hall out of a desire to see her son accepted as the rightful heir to the title of Hellistone and all that it stood for. As the son of a single woman of questionable heritage, he would have had difficulty making his way in the world. His social position would always have been in question. His acceptance into the schools of the *ton* would have been an impossibility. But as the acknowledged legal heir of Hellistone, he would be desirable not only in his own right, but also could be counted an asset to his country.

All of Eleanor's fears when she had discovered herself to be pregnant and destitute, before Miss Shappley had rescued her from an uncertain fate, rose to the surface as she watched her husband studying the boy. Her love for her child was the strength that held her days together. Her pride in his innate dignity and winsomeness gripped her throat, making speech impossible.

She waited, her heart fluttering with anxiety, her breath held by lungs immobilized by apprehension until at last Geoffrey said, "Welcome to Hellistone Hall, Phillip." He slowly extended his hand to his son. "I hope you will be happy here."

Even as he greeted the boy, he wondered at his ready acceptance of this woman's story. Something about her was appealing—a certain air of sadness. Suddenly he wanted to take back his words, to send these people far away, to a place where he would never see them. Their arrival would alter his life greatly, and he wasn't prepared for such change.

But the touch of the child's hand in his, and the confiding tone as Phillip agreed that he was sure he would enjoy Pentalwyn, drew Geoffrey's attention. He responded to the boy's hope that he would find a stable for his new pony.

"You ride, do you? That's . . . very nice." There was an awkward pause. Finally Eleanor made a motion to the woman who had entered the room with Phillip.

"My lord, this is Mrs. Ogden. She is my friend and companion and goes with me wherever I go." Eleanor lifted her chin, directing her challenge at the taciturn man standing opposite. Her lip curled in derision at the curt tilt of the earl's head as he acknowledged the introduction.

Once more silence filled the room as each party eyed

the other, waiting for someone to do or say something that would relieve the tension. Geoffrey was momentarily at a loss as to what to do next. His mind revolved around this unprecedented situation. That he could have married and forgotten, that he should have become engaged while married, that his unknown wife should appear from out of nowhere presenting to him an unlooked-for son, that he had to inform Lady Coddington of the whole—all were a series of events he would rather have lived without. At last he shrugged his shoulders, still silent. Chiswick would have to see the unwelcome party settled in a suite of rooms.

Unexpectedly, Mrs. Ogden made a remark about a piece of sculpture that stood on a malachite base in an alcove between two of the windows. She commented on its obvious antiquity, asking if it were Greek. Pleased to be able to turn his attention from the wife and child he had never known, the earl answered and was shortly involved in a brief discussion about his experiences in Greece the preceding year.

As the earl spoke with Mrs. Ogden, Eleanor moved to Phillip's side and put her hand protectively on the boy's shoulder. She leaned over to whisper in his ear, complimenting him on his deportment before his father.

"I don't think he likes me very much," Phillip replied, not taking his eyes from his father's face. "Do we really have to stay here, Mama? I'd rather go back home. Jemmy and Charlotte will be missing me. They might even forget me." He turned his eyes to his mother's face.

"No, Pip, darling, they would never forget you. We'll visit them one day, and you'll see that they remember you and still love you." She pulled the against her as she spoke. "This is home now, dearest. Your father will like you well enough once he gets to know you. He probably didn't expect such a handsome, strong boy and is too surprised to be very friendly."

"I 'spect you're right, but he didn't seem very glad

to meet me." The boy stood quietly, leaning against his mother.

Eleanor fell silent, too, wondering at her own temerity and the fortitude with which she had remained calm in the face of the earl's icy skepticism. She realized that he still had doubts about her veracity, despite the evidence of the marriage lines and the ring. Obviously, when he had inherited the title, he had become a man of great wealth. That combined with whatever prior experience he may have had since she had last seen him, had given him an attitude of distrust towards the world. It was completely possible that in introducing herself into his life and bringing this son to his notice, she might have done herself a greater disservice than that of remaining a quiet unknown. Nevertheless, no matter what the cost to herself, Phillip would benefit. For now, that was all that mattered.

Eleanor's thoughts were interrupted by the appearance of the elderly factotum. "My lord, you rang?"

"Chiswick, yes..." Geoffrey's casual conversation with Mrs. Ogden seemed to have taken his attention away from the matter at hand. "You will please see that... ah-h...Mrs...." He was at a loss for words to describe the unwanted trio, then decided abruptly that, for the moment, he must acknowledge the proof of his marriage. He started to give his directions to the butler once more. "Please see that my son and Mrs. Ogden are suitably quartered. My wife will join them shortly." Disregarding the surprise on the face of the old man, he turned to Eleanor to explain to her that he would appreciate her attendance upon him for a few moments before she retired to freshen herself.

Once Chiswick, followed by Phillip and Mrs. Ogden, had left the room, the earl slowly circled Eleanor, raising his quizzing glass to examine her. His eye missed nothing—the clenched hands with whitened knuckles, the flash of anger in her eyes, the slight flare of her nostrils, and above all, the rigidly held back, stiff as a board, refusing to bow to the discourteous scrutiny.

"Well, sir? Have you finished?" Eleanor's usually sweet voice was harsh as she met her husband's gaze.

"Quite well, madame. You'll do. One wife or the other, it makes no difference." He lowered the glass. "I need a wife. It might as well be you since you have already borne the heir." Once more he rang for a servant. "I ask that you be ready to meet my mother and our guests at half after the hour. It is now just three. That allows you thirty minutes."

Two minutes were left of the thirty minutes stipulated by Geoffrey when Eleanor rang for a servant to conduct her to her husband's presence. She and Mrs. Ogden had quickly discussed the coming presentation to the dowager countess and the unnamed guests who were enjoying the hospitality of the Earl of Hellistone.

"My dear Linnet," began Mrs. Ogden, using her nickname for Eleanor, "I do wish that you had waited until you had written this news to the earl. He looks to be a proud man and one who prefers to control events rather than be controlled." The imposing lady lifted her skirts as she backed up to the the fireplace in the spacious bedroom that had been assigned to Eleanor. "I think he was rather too stunned by your arrival and Phillip's to understand completely what was happening. But be assured that there will be one monstrous storm when he wakes up to the truth . . . and I do fear for your welfare when that happens."

"Lucretia, stop conjuring up more flights of fancy," Eleanor replied. "Keep them for the novels you read, if you please. Despite everything, he is a gentleman and will behave correctly." Eleanor turned huge golden eyes to her companion. A shadow of fear touched them for an instant then disappeared as she smiled. "You know, your imagination really sets me off. I could almost be-

lieve you when you look so mysterious and so prodi-
giously . . . pompous! Now rest your fantasies and let us
learn how to go about living in a palace such as this.
Call for a chambermaid to sit with Phillip when you're
ready to come down to dinner. Please allow me some
few minutes with Lord Hellistone before joining us."
Eleanor touched Mrs. Ogden's hand, half in plea, half
in comfort. "I think I will need your support by then."

She turned once more to view herself in the pier-glass
and straighten the folds of the amber gown she wore.
The modest décolletage revealed white shoulders and the
shadow of a delicately rounded breast. A double row of
darker amber velvet ribbons braided with pearls and topazes shaped the high waistline. A necklace of topazes,
each set in a circlet of seed pearls, reflected her glowing
eyes. Her hair was dressed simply in a knot bound with
pearls high on her head, with a few loose tendrils ca-
ressing her perfectly oval face.

When a rap at the door announced the arrival of her
escort, Eleanor picked up a sheer *mousseline de soie* scarf
embroidered with seed pearls in a tracery of leaves and
arranged it around her shoulders. She reminded her companion to take no longer than fifteen minutes before joining her, then followed the liveried footman down the
corridor.

She had no doubt that the coming meeting with Geoffrey would be even more difficult than the previous one.
Then she had the advantage of surprise. Because he had
no memory of her, he could marshal no defense. But
now his keen and incisive mind was sure to devise ar-
guments against her intrusion into his life. It was bound
to be unpleasant. The man who had been her savior that
spring day so long ago had become someone quite different. Eleanor doubted that the present earl would ever
succumb to overindulgence of brandy as an antidote to
any of life's disappointments. Nor would he respond to
a young damsel in distress with an act of chivalry, as

had the young Geoffrey de Maine.

But then, the young Eleanor would never have had the courage to make a claim upon another such as she was making upon Geoffrey now. True, it was her legal right to take her place at his side, but ethically she should be ready to step aside for his chosen bride.

Perhaps, though, she was doing him a favor. It was incomprehensible to Eleanor that he could have chosen the same woman who had treated him with such cruelty eight years ago. Whatever had happened in the years since then, it surely must have erased the meaning of love and tenderness from his character.

Eleanor had been following the footman automatically, lost in her thoughts. She was recalled to herself when his soft voice announced that they had reached the library. She responded with a smile of thanks and entered the room, her apprehension well hidden behind a calm expression and a dignified bearing.

"Well, at least you're punctual!" her husband greeted. If a glimmer of appreciation appeared in his eyes at her appearance, Eleanor was not aware of it.

She moved slowly across the carpet and sank gracefully into a chair before answering in a kind voice, "My Lord, you will learn that I am to be believed in whatever I say. I have no need of prevarication at any time." She watched him pour two glasses of wine from a gleaming crystal decanter. "Are we to drink a toast to our future together?"

"I hadn't thought of doing that, madam. I intended to offer you some Dutch courage against the coming meeting with your mother-in-law and my erstwhile fiancée." Without a modicum of emotion on his face, Geoffrey offered Eleanor the glass of wine. "To your very good health." He tossed back his own drink and replaced the glass on the silver salver with an abrupt movement. "I marvel at your sangfroid, my lady, to have arrived unbidden, announcing yourself and your son—"

"Your son also, my lord," Eleanor interrupted her husband.

"Yes, so you claim. Very well, my son." Geoffrey paced up and down the room as he spoke, unable to find a resting place. "To have announced yourselves so coolly, so calmly, so unexpectedly. What kind of reception did you look for?" He paused in his pacing, coming to a stop directly in front of Eleanor, studying her face as though looking for an answer to his question, wondering at her look of untouched beauty.

Eleanor sighed deeply, weighing her words. "I am prepared for any reception, sir, because I know myself to be in the right. You *did* marry me, and you *did* celebrate a brief . . . honeymoon with me, and you *did* leave me without any explanation. If I hadn't been rescued by Miss Shappley, I would in all likelihood have died, and Phillip would never have been born.

"You took me under your protection, my lord, and then you left me in a sorrier state than you had found me. I could think of no reception that would make me feel any worse than I felt at the moment when I discovered you to be no better than my despicable guardian."

Eleanor raised her eyes to the grave face before her. "With no thanks to you, I lived and was cared for and gave birth to a wonderful son for whom I am prepared to sacrifice my freedom in order that he should take his rightful place in the world. After all, is it really so much to give up for the grace and favor you could bestow upon us?" There was no mistaking the disdain of her last words.

Geoffrey's dark eyebrows flew up in surprise at the thought that his wife considered her situation a sacrifice. He contemplated her words, seeking to refute the import without losing his sense of superiority. After all, he was in command here. It was up to him to make her way difficult or easy and, in the face of the recalcitrant attitude she displayed, he would not be inclined to smooth her path.

"Do you expect 'grace and favor'?" he asked.

"Only for Phillip. *I* have no need of it. I have mentioned that Miss Shappley cared for me, but I didn't tell you that, upon her death, I became exceedingly wealthy. She left me her fortune, her jewels, and her three houses. You have no need to concern yourself with supporting me. In fact, I would be willing to add to *your* wealth a portion of mine should you wish to be paid for recognizing your son and myself." A cynical smile twisted her lips. She had thrown the offer at him as though it were a gauntlet, knowing the insult he would consider it.

The color drained from Geoffrey's face, then returned in a flush of rage high on his cheekbones. "If you were a man..."

"If I were a man, dear sir, I wouldn't be sitting here talking to you about our son."

Geoffrey turned away abruptly, his hands clenched at his sides, the knuckles white with the effort to refrain from taking his wife's slender shoulders and shaking them until he had disturbed her cool equanimity. She was causing his head to pound alarmingly. Never before could he remember feeling such rage at another's behavior. Yet, what was she doing that piqued him so? Why should she have this effect on him?

He took several deep breaths. "I think it would be easier for both of us, and for everyone else, if we try to remain civil to one another," he said. "I must speak shortly to my mother and Lady Coddington, and I don't wish you to be present. You will allow us time alone and then Chiswick will show you into the blue salon. I hope there will be no display of temperament on your part when you do meet them. It will be a shock to everyone—even more so than it was to me—to learn of your existence. How we shall conduct ourselves in the future is something that will take a deal of thought. I haven't yet decided what I shall expect of you."

"And just what does that mean, sir?"

"Why, that I might expect you to take up your duties as a complaisant wife in return for 'grace and favor.'"

With that the earl withdrew, leaving a fuming Eleanor behind.

Complaisant wife, is it? 'Grace and favor'! Well, her hair might not be red, but her temper could match his. Just let him try . . .

CHAPTER TWO

"MY DEAR ALVINIA, much as it pains me to deny myself the joy of becoming your husband, I cannot bring myself to commit bigamy." The earl was seated in a deeply cushioned wing chair, speaking to his deposed fiancée, moments after he had left Eleanor.

Cold blue eyes glittered with anger as the petite blonde clenched her fists in frustration. "This is impossible, Geoffrey. How can you be sure that she isn't some adventuress with trumped-up credentials? The child could be the son of some mountebank! How can you be so willing to accept them into your home and... and..." Her diatribe sputtered to an end as Geoffrey's expression of concern was replaced by a chilling reserve that told her she was asking questions that were not hers to ask.

Quickly she changed her tactics and sank to her knees in front of him, positioning herself so that her soft white bosom was exposed to his eyes in the deep décolletage of her dress. Looking at him beseechingly, she continued. "Oh, my love, we have waited so long to be together. I know I was to blame." With a graceful bend of her neck, she lowered her head as though still a shy young maiden. "I never should have let my parents sway me from my commitment to you, but now, when our happiness is so close, to have this—this—impostor arrive and disrupt our plans...." Two crystal teardrops formed in the corners of her eyes, and exquisitely modeled pouting lips drooped with a childlike quiver.

Geoffrey de Maine examined the woman kneeling so gracefully before him, a cynical twist distorting his mouth. It was a wonder that a woman of close to thirty could maintain an air of innocent youth. Her slight stature in no way detracted from the voluptuousness of the body she had so freely offered to him. Truly, he thought, the stage had lost a great actress in her. How naïve she must believe him to be, or how blind she was to his true feelings for her. She had been his choice of bride solely because she *wasn't* the innocent she liked to pretend to be. He was aware that he was not her only *cher ami;* she would allow him his freedom within their marriage with no questions asked. She would have had her freedom also, once she had given him an heir, and she would have been discreet about any liaisons she might have contracted once the heir was born. Having already been married, she would expect nothing more or less than she had had before, which suited him well. She was not unattractive, and she had shown him often enough that he was welcome in her bed. They would have rubbed along as well as most other married couples. Now, of course, there was no longer any possibility of such an alliance. He already had a wife.

"Don't throw yourself into the dismals, Alvinia. Your eyes will be all red, and I'm sure you wish to look your best when you meet my wife." He extended his hand, then stood, drawing her up from the floor.

"Oh, Geoffrey, I can't bear to lose you." Alvinia threw her arms around the earl's neck. He knew it was his fifty thousand a year that she would miss most of all. She pressed her body against his, seeking to arouse him. "Oh, dearest, don't send me away from you. There may yet be something that we can do to set aside this marriage, if it is truly such."

Geoffrey casually grasped the softly rounded arms and lifted them away from his neck. "You do this very well,

Alvinia, but we both know that our betrothal had nothing to do with love or other gentle feelings. It was . . . expedient for us to contemplate marriage. Since there was no one for whom I had strong feelings, our union would have suited. You may stay here at Pentalwyn for a few more days—I am not so rude a host that I would ask you to leave at once—but you and your mother will have to bring your visit to a close. In the meantime, I want no Cheltenham tragedies enacted. Is that clear?"

Heavy lids fringed with long blond eyelashes touched with kohl hid eyes filled with chagrin. Alvinia took a deep breath, waiting until she could speak without betraying the depth of her malevolence. When she finally spoke, her voice was as sweet and gentle as though she had just been given the news that the sun would shine this day.

"Of course, Geoffrey. I assure you that I will do my utmost to welcome your . . . wife. I'm sorry that you feel that my reasons for wanting to marry you did not include my love. You must know that my thoughts were ever with you, even when I was coerced into marrying Coddington. I prayed for you when you were in the army, always hoping that we would finally find our happiness with each other."

"Enough!" the earl interrupted rudely. "I know your prayers started at my brother's death, so don't try to play a game with me."

Not allowing her time to answer, Geoffrey went through the now-open door, leaving an enraged woman behind him.

Alvinia shuddered with anger. Finally, unable to control herself any longer, she picked up a delicate Sevres statue, held it in her hands for a moment as though feeling its heft, and then, with all the strength of which she was capable, threw it on the floor. The resultant explosion of sound brought a quick response from one of the liveried footmen on duty in the corridor.

Lady Coddington glanced at him calmly. "A statue fell off the table," she said. "See that this mess is cleaned up immediately." Leaving the startled servant to his work, she swept haughtily from the room.

Geoffrey found his mother strolling in the Long Gallery, enjoying the wealth of paintings displayed there. Lady Hellistone, now the dowager countess, was a gentle woman. She had married at a very young age and, although a widow and the mother of a son above thirty and a daughter ten years younger, she was under fifty-five years of age. Her reddish hair was lightly touched with strands of white, and her skin was soft and youthful. Despite giving the impression that she was a person of whimsical vacillation, that lady was capable of determination and resolution when the happiness of her children was concerned.

Imogene de Maine detested Alvinia. She had followed Lady Coddington's career while Geoffrey was serving in the army and was cognizant of her many affairs and her spiteful character. Lady Hellistone sincerely believed that life with Alvinia would be a hell on earth for Geoffrey. The reason why this woman had been twice chosen by her son was a complete mystery to the countess. She had credited him with enough acuity to distinguish gilt from gold, but apparently as far as women were concerned, he was still a babe.

Not even she, who loved him, was aware of the boredom and lack of meaning Geoffrey found in his life. It had driven him into the proposed marriage in the hopes that a change from bachelorhood to married ties would give life added meaning. He had never fallen madly in love—not since his first bout with Alvinia—so he understood himself to be incapable of such strong feelings. Without love, any woman would serve his needs—therefore the choice of his former love.

"Dear one," Lady Imogene greeted her son as he

walked towards her in the shadowed light of the long, high-ceilinged room. "Have you come to escort me to dinner?"

"Eventually, Mother," Geoffrey returned. "Come, let's sit down in this alcove. I have something to tell you." He drew her over to a deep window seat where they could view the walled rose garden. Once settled, he took her hands in his and studied them as though seeking an answer to some unknown problem.

A few moments passed quietly. Lady Imogene watched her son, waiting for him to open the conversation.

"You know, Mama, you have the gift of silence. I think you must be the only woman in the world who doesn't batter one with questions and chatter." He lifted gray eyes warm with love. "As you can tell, I'm having trouble finding the words to convey my news to you."

"Usually, my dear, the best way is to start at the beginning and tell it right through to the end."

"Yes, undoubtedly you're right about that. But it's so damned difficult to get started." He raised her hand to his lips and saluted her with a kiss. "A long time ago," he started, "I thought my great love was Alvinia—before she married Coddington, that is. Having never left Pentalwyn, except to go to school, until after I reached my majority, I was a very naïve young man. A real country bumpkin, you might say. Well, anyway, we were secretly betrothed, and she had promised to wed me by special license. I made all the arrangements and procured the license but, when I arrived at our meeting place two weeks later, she had already wed the baron. When I found out, I think I must have gone slightly mad. I had no one to talk to. None of my friends were nearby. Nor would I have confided in any of them, so great was my hurt. I must have withdrawn to the nearest inn and drowned my sorrows for several days. When I became aware of things once more, I found myself at a hostelry in bed with a woman." Geoffrey looked at his mother apologetically.

"Thinking she was no more than a light-skirt, I emptied my pockets of cash as remuneration for her services, then I made my way home. You know the rest of my story afterwards."

"Yes, my dear. . . . It's not such an unusual occurrence . . . young men, and you were still almost a boy . . . I really . . ." Lady Imogene tried to express comfort and understanding without really knowing why her son was disclosing such personal experiences to her.

"But Mother, what makes this different is that it seems I had married the girl who was in my bed, but I was so under the influence of the landlord's potion that I have no memory of the occasion."

"But, Geoffrey, how is that possible? All those years and you never remembered your *marriage?* And how do you know you *were* married?"

"My bride has arrived here at Pentalwyn."

"But why did she leave it until now? Why has she never contacted you? This sounds like one of Mrs. Radcliffe's stories."

"It's a long story, *ma mère,* but there's more you must know right now. She did not arrive here alone. She has brought my son with her."

"Your son?" Lady Imogene's voice was a faint sound in the spacious room. As though the news was too much for her to assimilate, she closed her eyes. "Are you sure?"

"When you meet him, you will see the similarity. In truth, he looks like his mother, but he has the de Maine eyes and our hair. A touch brighter red—but you always told me that mine darkened as I got older."

"Ummm, yes . . . Well, this is extraordinary news! Have you told Lady Coddington that she is deprived of the brideright of becoming a de Maine?"

Geoffrey wondered if there was a hint of—could it be malice in his mother's voice?

"Where did you have Chiswick put her?" his mother continued.

"Put her?"

"Of course. If she's your wife, she must have all the honors due her as Countess of Hellistone." Lady Imogene's eyes began to sparkle. "Yes, she should have the Elizabethan suite. It connects to yours, which is as it should be. Also, except for my rooms, it is the finest in the Hall.

"Tell me, Geoff, shall I like her?" she went on. "And my grandson, do you like him?" Without a pause the earl's mother began to consider the ramifications of their guest's presence at Pentalwyn. "Oh, dear, what shall we do about the betrothal ball? Will we be able to notify everyone in time?" She rose up from the velvet-covered seat, excitement running through her. This unknown could not possibly be as cold and calculating as Alvinia.

"Geoffrey, my dear, I don't think we should cancel the ball. Just change the reason for it. Instead of being held for the purpose of announcing your betrothal, we shall introduce your wife to our family and friends. I wonder if she has the right kind of gown. What is she like, Geoffrey? Is she presentable?"

Amazed and amused by his mother's response to the news of a daughter-in-law and a grandson, Lord Hellistone answered her questions, trying to describe the tall, slim woman who had come out of his forgotten past to present him with a son of whom he had had no knowledge. As he painted a picture of her dignity, her beauty, and her self-possession in so awkward a situation, his mother listened carefully to the tone of his voice and watched the expression on his face. She knew that the news was a terrible blow to Alvinia and that "that woman," as she labeled her, would try to prevent this heretofore unknown wife from spoiling her plans. If only there were one or two allies within the household who could help keep the harpy at bay, perhaps this affair would prove more felicitous than one could imagine.

Because Lady Imogene knew her son to be a generous,

kind, and loving person who was hiding behind an austere manner, she wished him to have a wife who would bring him the happiness he deserved. The arrival of a woman who had kept her own counsel for eight years presented a less-than-perfect opportunity to oust Alvinia from the scene. But if there was any possibility that the new countess might learn to love and be a comfort to Geoffrey, then Imogene de Maine would certainly see to it that the hoped-for circumstance was encouraged.

As mother and son followed their own thoughts, they made their way to the magnificent chamber to which Chiswick had directed the various members of the house party. They arrived just in time to hear Eleanor introducing herself to Alvinia in answer to that woman's discourteous demands to know who she was. A tranquil response was made, and then Eleanor turned from her rival to introduce Mrs. Ogden to the company.

That elderly lady had grown up in the theater and enjoyed exploiting the impact a singular appearance had upon one's audience. To that end, she had clothed her tall, imposing body in layers of diaphanous fabrics hung with strings of beads and pinned with brooches and all manner of jewels. Upon her head sat an oversized turban wound of flaming orange satin, draped with strands of pearls and semiprecious stones. Atop the whole, three ostrich plumes nodded graciously to all present. Wisps of curly gray hair crept out from under the monstrous headgear, framing a chubby pink face in which a pair of twinkling eyes bade all and sundry to enjoy the sight she presented.

Instead of putting off the several ladies and gentlemen present, her appearance seemed to attract them. Her hearty laugh, humorous asides, and sincere interest in those with whom she spoke won many admirers.

The earl's arrival, accompanied by his mother, drew Eleanor's eyes. She watched as he made his way across the room to her side. His well-built figure, clothed in a midnight-blue superfine tailcoat, obviously from the workrooms of Weston of London, stood out in the roomful of people. His fitted trousers which outlined his muscular legs, the double-breasted waistcoat of pale blue and cream stripes, and the crisply starched cravat tied in a restrained manner all added to the fashionable appearance he made. Eleanor's breath caught in her throat as she gazed at his handsome face. His extraordinary gray eyes were so like Phillip's. The crown of dark reddish hair, cut in a casual *coup de vent* style and streaked from the sun, looked so crisp that she wanted to touch it.

Was it possible that she had lain in this man's arms so long ago? Was the tremor in her knees a result of her memories of that one night of passion, or because of the role she would now be called upon to play? A becoming flush suffused her countenance when Geoffrey raised a questioning eyebrow.

"Madam," he greeted her, giving no hint of the conversation they had had less than an hour before. "You look very well." His voice dropped to a whisper as he commanded, "Be so good as to let me introduce you to my mother." Without waiting for her to lay her hand on his forearm, he took her fingers and tucked them into his crooked elbow. "Don't pull away, my lady, or you will spoil the welcoming picture I wish to present to our guests. We must try to behave in a way that incites envy of our situation, not ridicule."

"My lord, I am yours to command." A hiss of anger touched Eleanor's words.

"Yes, I know," was the bland response.

A *sotto voce* response, too soft for the earl to hear, was made to the effect that there would be more of this matter in the future, then, as she was brought to a stop before the earl's mother, she said, "My lady, I have waited a long time for this pleasure." As she sank into a deep curtsy to convey her respect, Eleanor peeked up at the sweet face that looked at her with ... could it be kindness and welcome?

"My dear, come and let me kiss you. I cannot tell you how pleased I am." Lady Imogene's eyes slid to Alvinia's face and noted the fury on it. "We shall have a nice long coze after dinner. Geoffrey, she is every bit as lovely as you told me. Now, do your duty and introduce her to everyone before Chiswick announces dinner. I know you will want her by your side during the evening, but"—she tapped her son's wrist playfully with her fan— "you must be ready to allow her to attend me later."

The smile that always appeared in his eyes when he dealt with his mother changed the earl's appearance completely. The cold, staid demeanor that was habitual with him warmed to a friendlier, younger look. For a moment he resembled the young man who had married Eleanor on that April day eight years ago.

"Yes, *ma mère*, you shall talk with her as much as you like." He started to move away, drawing Eleanor with him. "We will answer to everyone who has the bad taste to ask that I suffered a bout of amnesia and so lost track of you. Which is the truth, thus simpler to speak. Since the betrothal was bruited about in the newspapers, the situation will be awkward, but if we stress the happy ending for you and me, we should manage to avoid an excessive amount of gossip. With difficulty, I have convinced Alvinia not to announce her breaking heart." His words took on a cynical tone. "I'm sure that she will be satisfied with a generous gift and continued recognition as a friend of the Earl and Countess Hellistone, as well as an occasional invitation to some of our balls and routs."

By the time he had finished speaking, they had arrived at the side of the deposed fiancée. With a loving look, she wrapped her hands around Geoffrey's free arm, and smiled at Eleanor with cordial detestation.

"So this is the long-lost countess, Geoffrey. You must

have been enjoying your life immensely to have remained concealed for such a length of time, my dear. Did you suffer some kind of reversal to make you appear so unexpectedly?" Alvinia's words were spoken in a most solicitous manner.

"No, my lady, only the thought that you might be the unknowing victim of an act of bigamy brought me here. Even though neither party was aware of such a happening, it would have put you forever beyond the pale had I permitted your wedding to take place. I could not bear the thought of an innocent woman suffering such a fate." Eleanor's eyes gleamed with golden lights of fury, belying her tranquil manner.

"How kind of you to have been so solicitous of my well-being." A pouting mouth spoke the words, but the tone made certain that Eleanor knew her thoughtfulness was not appreciated.

"I think my wife showed every kindness to have rushed to your side as she did," Geoffrey interposed. "The necessity of preventing such a heinous deed, no matter how innocently enacted, was her first concern. You should thank her for her actions." A hint of laughter showed in the gray eyes. Eleanor caught her breath at the sight. It was as if a charming, mischievous boy was lurking behind the reserved mask.

"If this woman is truly your wife..." Alvinia's protuberant blue eyes seemed to promise some malign fate.

Tall, dark-haired Eleanor drew herself up, intending to convey challenge in her very posture. Let Alvinia just dare to continue her insulting remarks!

"Alvinia." Warning was implicit in the earl's one word. He waited a moment, then turned to Eleanor. "My dear, I think we must greet more of our guests before we may go into dinner." He gripped his wife's elbow and urged her forward as he cautioned Alvinia with a glance.

For the first time since he had returned to England after the war, he found himself looking forward to the next few weeks. Suddenly his boredom had been done away with. Life was once more filled with challenge.

"Your choice of a lady-love disappoints me, sir," Eleanor commented. "I cannot think it a good reflection upon myself that you should be so errant in settling upon such a one as my replacement." The words were expressed without emphasis, the inference being that the lady was merely making conversation and the topic was of passing interest.

"Ah, but I had not the privilege of recalling you to mind, my lady. Perhaps after tonight I shall have a better model to use as a pattern. My dear, may I make you acquainted with my very good friend, Jeremy Broadbent. Jeremy, my wife."

Eleanor extended her hand to the young gentleman just introduced. "A pleasure, sir. You have a look of the military about you. Did you serve with Wellington?"

"How did I give myself away?" Twinkling brown eyes in a cherubic face looked approvingly at Eleanor. "If I had your husband's dashing manner, I might have thought that had betrayed me, but, as it is, you must tell me what I did wrong."

A delicious trill of laughter broke from Eleanor's parted lips. Something about this short, erect man seemed to set her at ease. His was the first face she had seen that held a sincere welcome. Even when she had given thought to the difficulties she would encounter in introducing herself to her husband and his household, Eleanor had not prepared herself for the strain of holding herself aloof from the multitude of emotions she was arousing in the various persons she was meeting. Here, at least, was someone who was welcoming her as the wife of his friend. She was more than grateful for his acceptance.

"It was an impression of the moment, sir," she said. "A certain air of valor and knightliness . . . as though you would ride *ventre-à-terre* to save the day, if need be."

Geoffrey joined the laughter her answer evoked. "And

so he would. And many a scrape did he find himself in that called for someone else to ride to *his* rescue without thought of the consequences." The lightly spoken words merely hinted at the deep affection the two friends shared. Each had saved the other's life more than once, and they had looked out for one another during that horrendous last battle, Waterloo.

There were but a few more people to whom Eleanor was introduced before Chiswick entered to announce that dinner was served. The young countess found herself being escorted into the magnificent dining room on the arm of Lord Trevellyan, her husband's uncle and the ranking peer present. They conversed easily together about the beauties of spring and rose gardens and the quiet of the country.

As the old gentleman seated her, he gave her a long look from under his shaggy eyebrows. "Mystery here, eh? Look like a nice enough gel. Good figger. Like you better than that other hoity-toity miss. You'll do, m'dear, you'll do." At the end of his astonishing statement, Lord Trevellyan turned away to find his place at the table, leaving a stunned Eleanor behind him.

The dinner lasted for some two and a half hours. Course followed course, each one more elaborate than the last. Several removes were presented for the delectation of the guests—three soups began the meal and were followed by pike in the German way, fricassee of lobster, several savories, and two jellies. These were followed by calf's-foot jelly, roasted beef, broiled mutton, and boiled turkeys stuffed with capons. Several *petits-pâtés*, a fricandeau of veal, carrot pudding, tender green peas with mint, parsnips in butter, and boiled greens preceded whipped syllabub, apple charlotte, three kinds of gateaux, and fresh strawberries with Devonshire cream. Champagne was served throughout the meal, helping to create a gaiety that might not have been felt otherwise due to the unusual circumstances of Eleanor's presence.

At a signal from the dowager countess, the ladies arose from the table and withdrew to the salon, there to while away their time in conversation and gossip, leaving the gentlemen to their port and cigars.

Eleanor managed to avoid contact with Alvinia for most of the remainder of the evening, although she was the recipient of several killing looks. Protected by Mrs. Ogden, who quickly entered any conversation that impinged upon her friend's privacy, the "bride" drifted from one guest to another, smiling prettily and giving away nothing. When the ladies were joined by the gentlemen, Eleanor quickly excused herself, being exhausted by the day's events. She was conducted graciously to the door of her chamber by her husband, who allowed that he would not inflict himself upon her for the next few nights, giving them a chance to know one another better before resuming their interrupted enjoyment of married bliss.

Eleanor's eyes widened in alarm. The earl had given her notice that he might assert his rights as husband, but she had hoped to hold him at bay for some several months. In the years since they had spent that one night together, she had allowed no other man to become so close that intimacy might have been the result. The one night of her life that had taught her all she knew of the physical side of marriage had left bitter feelings, despite the enjoyment she had found in Geoffrey's embrace.

Now, once more faced by the handsome, charming man who had held her in his arms and had left her *enceinte,* she felt again the tug at her senses that produced unaccountable sensations in the pit of her stomach and a certain dryness of her mouth. Her tongue touched her lips cautiously as she stared into the silvery eyes. Trembling, she offered him her hand, trying to mask the effect of his words with a composed "Thank you and goodnight."

She pushed open the door to her suite, turning to close it behind her, only to find herself standing within the circle of the earl's arms. "Sir..." she began to object.

"I think it only right that we begin to renew our acquaintance with each other, Eleanor. And what better way then a kiss between husband and wife?"

His head descended and his lips took possession of hers. Her body sagged against his, and her hands clutched at his lapels for support. Even as she held on to him, his arms tightened around her, pulling her close to his muscled chest, igniting flames within her that she had never imagined existed. His moist warm mouth moved against hers, brushing, sipping, seeking for the softness and secrets there. Her lips parted, helplessly, giving entry to his urgent tongue, allowing the shadow of passion to send her into a mindless state of sensation. She seemed to have lost the power to breathe. Just as she thought she would die of asphyxiation, the earl lifted his head and held her with his eyes.

"You're very lovely, Eleanor." His voice trembled slightly. "Don't turn away from me." He lifted his hand to her chin, and held her still. "Come, let me sip your nectar again. It's the sweetest that's ever touched my lips."

"No... Please..." Her words died away as, once more, his mouth claimed hers. Again she was captured by the tide of passion. Her mouth yielded to his. Her tongue answered his as her arms clasped him tightly to her.

Geoffrey felt her body shake with the storm of emotion that swept through her. Without letting go, he reached behind him to turn the key in the lock, successfully blocking entry to any who might follow them into the room. Slowly he began to caress her body, stroking the line of her backbone, the swell of her hips. His hands moved to her breast, pushing the amber fabric aside as he attempted to reach the rosy tips.

A sigh of sound formed words. "Oh, Geoffrey..." It was half-plea, half-protest.

"Yes, Eleanor . . . come . . . let me carry you." He barely lifted his lips from hers as he answered, not wishing to relinquish his advantage. His one arm held her shoulders as the the other lowered to clasp her legs, lifting her easily to hold her against his body as he strode from the sitting room through the boudoir into the bedroom. A banked fire in the fireplace was the only light in the dim chamber, casting deep shadows around the tester bed. Eleanor felt Geoffrey lower her to the mattress, still keeping her captive to his mouth and arms. She tried to push him away, but was seduced into surrender by his skilled attack. Delicately, he let go of her lips, moving his mouth to the side of her neck. With his tongue he tasted her, first flicking the sensitive skin, then mouthing the area with her lips. The sensations that began at the point of contact moved to the core of her body, filling her with an aching need, pushing all thoughts of the consequences out of her mind.

Somewhere in her consciousness, she was aware of her husband's hands undressing her gently, discarding her clothing piece by piece. Soon she felt the warmth of his hard body against hers, his hands still stroking, palpating, arousing her. His mouth took command of one pale breast, shocking a gasp of pleasure from her. Words became moans, pleading for surcease, exclaiming in delight. At last he covered her body with his, gently eased her legs apart, and entered her. It was as though it were the first time all over again. A sharp pain, a minor discomfort, but then a burst of sensation that caused her to cry out in wonder. His mouth and hands continued to coax wave after wave of thrills from her as his plunging body brought her to the precipice of wonder. Suddenly the scintillation of lights burst in her mind as tremors of feeling caught her in a vortex that started deep within her being and flooded her every nerve ending to the tips of her fingers and the soles of her feet. A duet of sound arose from them. They had achieved that moment of celebration together, had become one for a fleeting time.

Minutes later, when Eleanor returned to herself, she found herself still held by Geoffrey, his hand moving over her body in a soothing, gentling fashion. He murmured sounds, words that were nonwords but calmed at the same time that they enchanted. Bemused by his whispers, Eleanor lay quiescent, relishing the languor that had overcome her in the aftermath of the passion they had just shared.

But then, as she allowed her mind to replay the scene from the beginning, her lassitude slowly began to change until suddenly it burgeoned to fury. He had taken her without a thought for herself. He had known that she wished to delay the time when they would live as husband and wife until they had become more familiar with each other. She felt no better than any light-skirt whom he might have petitioned in his travels. She shrugged herself out of his arms, reaching for a coverlet to use as a wrap, knowing that part of her anger was at her own weakness. To have succumbed to his blandishments, to have responded to his magnetic virility, brought her down to his level. She wanted to throw things, to scream with rage, to bury her head in the pillow and weep. Instead she withdrew from the man who had given her pleasure without giving her the sense of self that was so important to her.

"What is it, sweetling? Don't pull away from me, wife. We are just coming to know one another." Geoffrey's voice was soft with sated passion.

"You are despicable. Get out of my bed."

"But why, love? Was it not as good for you as for me?"

"That has nothing to do with anything. You knew I wished to wait. You could have allowed me the dignity of getting to know you better instead of taking me without feeling, without love."

"Oh, no, not unfeelingly. I felt very well, I thought."

A hint of laughter came through the words.

"Don't laugh at me you . . . you . . . viper. You're like any other licentious beast, not even waiting a decent length of time before claiming what you consider yours by right."

"You are my wife. You showed me the lines yourself."

"That didn't give you the right to—to—"

"To make love to you? Why do you object? You enjoyed it as much as I did." Geoffrey was showing signs of impatience.

"You said you wouldn't rush me . . . that you would give me time to get to know you. It's indecent, to be taken like a—like a—"

"At least we know that we don't find each other distasteful, my dear. We shall find great pleasure in bed together, if nowhere else."

"Oh, how can you be so crude as to speak of such intimacies when you . . . I . . ." Eleanor found the idea of further shared pleasures with Geoffrey too exciting and too frightening to contemplate. It would mean a return to that emotionally dependent state that she had suffered for months after his betrayal of her. Somehow she must turn his lust away from her. She couldn't allow him to take her so casually. It meant too much to her. She knew herself to be falling deeply in love with her husband. If he didn't return her feelings, she didn't wish to share an intimate life with him.

"If you were honest with yourself, my lady, you would not pretend such a sensibility about passion. It can relieve boredom, solace the lonely, bring sleep to the weary, enliven a dull existence, and otherwise enhance the long hours of the night . . . or day. Think on it, dear wife. You must expect to pay some kind of recompense for your place here at Pentalwyn." By now the loving voice had turned cold.

Geoffrey swung his feet to the floor and moved away

from the bed. In the flickering illumination of the fire, his body was magnificent—flawlessly muscled, with broad shoulders tapered to a narrow waist and long, well-shaped legs. The strong lines were broken by a puckered scar that reached from his left shoulder blade down and around to his waist.

Eleanor's breath hissed at the sight, knowing that he must have been close to death after taking such a wound. Her arm reached out involuntarily, as though to touch the scar, but was unnoticed by an angry Geoffrey.

"I trust you will forgive me if I don't spend more time in this desert of passion, milady. It makes for a rather chilly bed."

"I'm sure you will find warmer climes elsewhere, sir." Tears had begun to form in Eleanor's eyes, but she turned her back to him, refusing to allow him to see how hurt and distraught she was.

The click of the door announced her solitude. My God, what stirred in her that she felt both desire for and detestation of him? When he touched her she melted . . . she wanted only to be in his arms and—but he used her as a plaything. He had done it once before, but she was a child then . . . now she knew what happened when one gave oneself into the keeping of a man. No more! He may want her, but she'd do her damnedest to keep him away from her. He could take solace with his doxy . . . and leave her to herself.

CHAPTER THREE

"COME OVER HERE, Phillip. Let me straighten your jacket." Lucretia Ogden addressed the child, who had been running around the paneled room. "Your Papa will surely take offense if you appear before him looking like some kind of hobbledehoy."

"Is he going to take me riding with him today?" The boy stood patiently before the elderly lady to be tugged at and patted until his clothes had the orderliness she gauged appropriate. "He said at breakfast that he would take me in his curricle when he went to the village."

"You'll find out all in good time, my dear." A pat on the head told him she had finished with him. "Now take yourself off to the garden, but don't go into the maze. It's too cold for you to get lost in there today." She watched with a fond expression as the boy ran exuberantly towards the door. "Now, mind what I say, Pip, or it will go poorly for you."

As the child went out the door, Mrs. Ogden sighed and stretched, looking around her at the sumptuous salon that was part of the suite assigned to her. The exquisite moldings, hand-carved in the shapes of all manner of fruits, were picked out in gold against walls of a delicate green. On the floor was a carpet of silk and wool from the workshop of the master weavers of Aubusson. The various chairs and sofas were a mixture of French styles upholstered with tapestries in muted colors depicting birds and mythological beasts.

The lady was drawn from her contemplation by a quick knock at the door and then the appearance of the young Countess Hellistone.

"Good morning, Lucretia, I've come to take Pip for a walk." Eleanor walked over to her companion and touched her cheeks lightly with a kiss. "Did you sleep well last night?"

"Divinely, my dear. One can say nothing bad about the beds here. Every comfort . . . and hot bricks and the fire kept up all night. Such courtesy, such thoughtfulness."

"Yes, I suppose one could think that, although I'm sure they would show the same thoughtfulness to any stranger within the gates." Eleanor seated herself on one of the sofas. "Where's Pip?"

"Oh, he was off shortly before you entered. He went to look for his Papa, who promised him a ride in a curricle."

Eleanor shivered and drew her shawl more closely about her. "Lucretia, have I done the right thing, bringing Pip here and interfering with the earl's marriage to that woman? I'm beginning to wish I'd never seen the announcement in the paper. We were going on so comfortably in our little house. And now I think I've created greater problems for myself."

"Don't be foolish. How can you even think such a thing? You know how important it is to Pip to have his father acknowledge him. Even if you find this life less to your liking than you had hoped, you must agree that your son can be happy. Already he gets on with the earl." Mrs. Ogden's billowy robes puffed up as she sank down on the couch next to Eleanor. "You're merely suffering a megrim because this is all so new to you. I want to remind you, my dear, that Miss Shappley thought you every bit as elegant as any woman she had ever met. She ensured that you would be able to conduct yourself properly in any situation and left you her fortune as a signal of her regard. Remember how unsure of yourself you were when we found you? So sick, so alone?

"You grew well again under her ministrations and finally came to trust us. I remember how confused you were and unable to understand why your husband had left you as he did. I watched your affection for him change to hatred, and then to something less passionate than that. Now, Eleanor, you will have to resolve these feelings, for Pip's sake as well as your own. What do you feel when you're with the earl? Love, hatred, or disdain?"

"I . . . don't know. We haven't spent much time together these past few days."

Eleanor hadn't revealed to Mrs. Ogden the intimacies her husband had shared with his bride the night of their arrival. Since then, he had virtually ignored her. Her body continued to act the traitor, crying out for his firm length next to hers, but her mind refused to approach him to make peace.

"Except at the dinner table and after, I haven't really seen him to speak to since the afternoon we arrived. He—I—I feel a response to him that I thought dead, and it frightens me. If he were to know that, I am afraid that he would use it against me to control Pip.

"He is so uncaring," Eleanor continued. "The first night we were here, he conducted me to my rooms and spoke to me as though . . . as though I were a woman of the streets. He was . . . without delicacy, without understanding of my feelings. I suspect he thinks I have had other lovers since he and I were together—which he can't or won't remember. If Pip weren't so like him with his gray eyes and red hair, he wouldn't recognize us, despite our marriage lines." A white hand with long, tapering fingers pushed at the weight of the knot of dark hair atop her head. "He infuriates me at the same time

that he awakens me. Oh, Lucretia, I don't know what
to do!"

"Why, the best would be to take things as they come.
I sense a certain ardor in his regard for you. The first
order of the day is to be rid of that terrible Lady Coddington and her mother. I happened to have a chat with
your mama-in-law yesterday—a very nice lady, that—
and she let on to me that she is exceedingly relieved that
there can no longer be a marriage between that one and
my lord. Lady Imogene expressed complete astonishment
that her son could have attempted to ally himself with a
woman who played such a trick upon him as to jilt him
the way she did. She thinks the world of her son, but
says he has changed beyond recognition since he was
thrown over by the very same woman he planned to
marry . . . before you arrived.

"Shortly after the incident, he begged his father to
buy him a set of colors, which the old earl did, and
Geoffrey went off to fight the French. He lived abroad
for several years, returning here only after his father and
older brother were lost at sea. He was severely affected
by the losses under his comand, Lady Imogene learned
from Mr. Broadbent. That, combined with his unfortunate love affair, had given him a wary eye toward marriage." Mrs. Odgen picked at a plate of bonbons as she
spoke. "Hardly ever tells anyone what he's up to, but
he's very thoughtful of his mama. Ah, me, but I do
ramble on. You must do what you think is best, Linnet,
but don't make any hasty decisions. I'm sure you will
win him if you give yourself the chance."

"Win him! I can't imagine why you should think that
is something I desire."

"Don't tell *me* a tale, my girl. You said he awakens
you. That's the first step—and sometimes the most important. If *you* can awaken him now, why, then your life
would be cream for the cat!" Mrs. Ogden gave Eleanor
a quick hug. "I think you should try to put yourself in

your husband's way as much as possible, if only to establish your right to be here. Lady Coddington should be invited to leave at the first opportunity. He'll do that only when he notices you enough to want you alone, without the reminder of his betrothal."

"Don't be ridiculous, Lucretia. I couldn't...Do you think I could?" A tide of color rose to Eleanor's cheeks. "No, there's no sense even trying. I would only leave myself in the same case as before. I trusted him, and look what happened."

"Have you spoken to your belle-mère?" A sly look appeared on Mrs. Ogden's round face. "Perhaps you should ask her for her thoughts on the matter. You might be surprised at what she has to say."

"I'm sure she'd rather not have heard of me at all. After all, who am I but some nobody her son happened upon?"

"Well! If I ever thought to hear you sound so self-pitying, Eleanor Glyndon de Maine! You're the daughter of a respectable English lady who was the daughter of a baronet. Just because your father was a wastrel doesn't make your birth any the less. After all, he *was* the youngest son of a youngest son of a marquess. It's just too bad that there were so many sons and daughters in the family that you seem to have been forgot by your aunts and uncles. But your heritage was a good one, and you exchanged it for a better one. Now, I don't want to hear you whining about being a nobody anymore. *You* are a countess, my girl, or had you forgot? And you rank higher than that Lady Codface who was only the wife of a baron, and not such a desirable one at that!"

Eleanor smiled in response to Mrs. Ogden's vehemence. "You are so good to me and for me, Lucretia. I don't know yet what I shall do for certain, but I shall talk to Geoffrey's mama." She arose from the sofa and walked to the window. "One would hardly know that I am a woman of twenty-six. In every other way, I have no difficulty in coming to decisions. But now I feel a mere slip of a girl with no experience to call upon and no knowledge of the right thing to do."

"Don't spend too much time worrying about it, just do as I suggested. Take each day as it comes. Things will work out." As she finished encouraging Eleanor, Mrs. Ogden swore under her breath that, if things didn't work out, her name wasn't Lucretia Ogden.

"Why don't you find Lady Imogene," Mrs. Ogden suggested. "She's anxious to speak with you and may have some good advice to give. Go along now, like a good child."

Eleanor started to laugh. "Really Lucretia... good child indeed."

"Well, so you are to one of my years."

"Very well, old lady, I'm gone." With a smile and a feeling of hopefulness, Eleanor left the room. She passed along the broad corridor and down the impressive double-winged staircase. Once in the main hall, she paused for a moment, sure that she would find Geoffrey's mother in the conservatory caring for her favorite orchids, but Eleanor was unsure of the exact location. No footmen were about to offer directions so she made a choice of doors and began to wander from one room to another.

She had quite forgotten the vastness of the Hall. *Palace* would be a better word. There were some forty or fifty public rooms, sixty bedrooms, a ballroom, several kitchens, a suite for the nursery of five bedrooms plus a schoolroom and a playroom, and finally, countless servants' rooms at the top of the house.

That didn't include the Long Gallery, the great hall, or the conservatory, any of which were large enough to encompass the whole of Miss Shappley's smallest house. An army of servants kept everything in order and included cooks, housekeepers, steward, butler, underbutler, valets, wine steward, dressers, nursemaids, tweenies, upstairs maids, parlormaids, footmen, gardeners, beaters, porters, stablehands, grooms, bailiff, huntsmen, and others too numerous to mention. The estate was some fifty thousand acres and included a village, a fishing port, several farms, a tin mine, and two small offshore islands.

The day before, the dowager countess had instructed Mrs. Quince, the senior housekeeper, to conduct the new countess through Pentalwyn, its outbuildings and some of the gardens. It had taken four hours just to circumnavigate the lower floor, so varied were the rooms, ornaments, furniture, fixtures, and paintings. When the housekeeper had asked about Eleanor's preferences in preparing the menus and giving directions for the conducting of the household, the younger woman recommended that Lady Imogene continue to hold the reins in her hands, for the time being.

"Oh, but my lady," Mrs. Quince responded, somewhat taken aback by this abrogation of duty, "her ladyship informed me that she would be removing to the dower house just as soon as she saw you were easy in your position here. I do believe you had better discuss this with her, if you don't mind my taking the liberty to advise you, my lady."

Eleanor almost looked around to see the "my lady" Mrs. Quince was addressing before she realized it was herself, Eleanor Glyndon de Maine, Countess Hellistone.

As she wandered through the many rooms, trying to find the conservatory, Eleanor pondered on the changed circumstance of her life. Never once in all her twenty-six years had she ever thought to be the mistress of so imposing a home. Never had she dreamed that the man she married was of the nobility. She was unimpressed by the ostentation, but was not sure she would fit in with the type of life she had read was the way members of the *haut ton* lived.

She was moving slowly through one of the minor parlors, her eyebrows twisted in thought, when a chill voice saluted her.

"Good morning, Lady de Maine." The slightly protuberent ice-blue eyes of the earl's erstwhile betrothed raked her over.

"Why, Lady Coddington, how nice to see you this morning." She'd be damned if she'd lower herself to discourteous behavior. "I'm looking for the conservatory. Can you direct me?"

"What on earth would you want there, madam?" The words were spoken as if to a servant.

Holding her temper in tight check, Eleanor explained in a soft voice that she was looking for the dowager countess.

"She told me she wanted nothing to do with you," was the response. "I should think you would be ashamed to show your face here after trying to insinuate yourself into this family as though you belonged. No better than you should be—and how you managed to find a legal marriage document with which to bamboozle—"

"Lady Coddington!" Icicles dripped from Eleanor's voice. "I think, for the sake of all of us, you should hold your tongue. I do not have to answer to you for anything. The earl accepts me as his wife and the mother of his son. Much as I regretted putting you at such a disadvantage, it was far better for it to have happened before you wed than after. You might have found yourself no more than the mistress of the earl, acknowledged or otherwise, carrying a bastard child." Her voice became sweeter than honey. "Truly, you should get down on your knees to thank me, my lady, not revile me." Eleanor waited for the vituperation she was sure would follow.

"Why, you—" A look of such hatred distorted the blond woman's face that Eleanor felt the hair on the nape of her neck stir in some primitive way. Alvinia's voice became hoarse with emotion. "Do you honestly think that Geoffrey will give me up just because you are here? You won't win. You . . . you . . . *I* will be Countess of

Hellistone, so enjoy your short time in the position. There are many ways to—"

"Do you threaten me, Lady Coddington?" Eleanor stared at her rival's twisted face, no longer showing the smooth good looks that ordinarily were Alvinia's.

"I warn you, madam, what is mine, I keep. And never doubt that Geoffrey will find a way out of the coil he's in."

"But my dear Lady Coddington, I think you mistake. Geoffrey was never yours. He has been mine all these years, and now I believe he finds himself satisfied in that situation. You should really take a new accounting of your position here. You no longer have a prospective husband in Geoffrey."

Eleanor took a seat and arranged her skirts carefully as she spoke. "Of course, it's always possible that he might set you up in your own little cottage in St. John's Wood, or some other out-of-the-way place where he would be able to call at his leisure. But I wish you to know that I shall make certain he will have very little time for such activities. Prepare yourself to spend many lonely hours while you await his coming."

Eleanor bestowed a gracious smile upon her enemy, concealing behind it a wish to tear the clothes off the woman and throw her out the door.

Unaware that there was a witness to the meeting between the two women, Alvinia approached Eleanor. "You cow—how dare you!" Her face was livid with anger. She raised a hand to strike her rival's face when her eye was caught by a movement near the door. Suddenly her hand dropped, and a sickly smile appeared on her lips. "Geoffrey, Geoffrey, did you hear? Are you going to let this . . . this . . ."

"'This' is my wife, Alvinia. I believe you are a trifle distraught. I'm sure we will forgive you should you feel the need to retire from the company for the rest of the day." The earl moved to his wife's side and took her arm in his as though they were the best of companions. "My mother is awaiting your presence, my dear. Let us leave Alvinia. She will do better by herself." Eleanor could almost swear there was some warmth in Geoffrey's silvery gray eyes. "Chiswick will see that your dinner is served in your room, Alvinia. Your mama is awaiting you. I'm sure you'll feel much better by tomorrow." The steel of command came through the gently expressed suggestion.

Without another word Alvinia hurriedly took leave of them. Her eyes promised retribution to the countess, but she was too cautious in Geoffrey's presence to give voice to that promise.

Sighing with satisfaction that the unpleasant scene was finally over, Eleanor carefully removed her arm from Geoffrey's. She had been taut with effort to hold back the inner trembling his touch had begun. In the eight years since he had awakened her body, she had never relaxed her vigilance enough to allow such response. . . . Or had it been that there was only one man to whom she could respond like this? Last night had shown her the power he held over her. He mustn't know—not until he felt something more than the curious half-regard she sensed in him. It would give him too much control over her should he even guess at the tumultuous stirring she felt in his company.

"I hate scenes," she said abruptly. "And your fiancée. . . I don't know what else to call her"—she explained in answer to his look of annoyance—"seems to enjoy them. I suppose you dote on her, to have wished to marry her?"

"I wouldn't say 'dote.' But, not knowing that I was already married, what else was I to do? Besides, she has certain . . . assets."

Eleanor felt an almost irresistible impulse to smack the sly smile from her husband's face. Could he be enjoying the whole contretemps? Could he—was it likely that he was relieved to have been freed from that importunate female? No, she must be imagining. It would be too much to hope for.

Geoffrey added, "And my mother has been urging me to set up my nursery."

"Naturally you always listen to your mother?" Eleanor refused to allow her wishful thoughts to interfere with their half-banter, half-serious speech. "You did tell me that you had come to escort me to my belle-mère, did you not?"

"I believe I mentioned it." Geoffrey moved closer to his wife, reaching out to catch her chin before she could move away. "You're quite lovely. I could have done worse than marry you. Are you in a pucker at the thought of spending time alone with Mama?" He let his right hand edge around her waist and gently drew her closer.

"I . . . why, of course not. She is all that is amiable." Eleanor found it more difficult to breathe. Geoffrey's hand was like a burning coal through the layers of her percale dress, even with its underslip and petticoat. She lifted heavy eyelids and found her eyes caught by the intense look in his. She felt herself sway towards him and put her hands on his shoulders to steady herself. From there it was but the matter of an instant before they had stolen around his neck as he bent forward to take her lips in a kiss at once gentle and passionate.

She forgot her surroundings, forgot that she had expressed a desire for him to leave her alone, forgot that she was a responsible woman of six-and-twenty. She gave herself up totally to the incredibly satisfying, sensuous, seductive sweetness of his kiss. Her lips parted under the pressure of his. The touch of his tongue against hers sent a thrill to the center of her being. She answered his questing with her own touches, pressing her body against his as though to absorb his essence into her. Lost in the wonder of sensations so newly awakened, she was for the moment unaware of his hand delicately cupping her breast, rubbing against the soft curves protected by her dress. When her body awoke to the delight of his hand, she responded with a soft growl and rose up on her toes to give him easier access to herself.

"I cannot help myself. You captivate me," he whispered as his lips left her mouth and moved first to her ear, then nibbled down the side of her neck to the hollow of her throat, creating waves of excitement in her. His left hand pushed at the lawn fichu, exposing the shadow between her breasts. He had just placed a kiss on the white skin when a cautionary cough brought his head up. Still holding Eleanor tightly against his lean body, he turned his eyes to the door.

"Chiswick. You wished to see me?" His voice was as casual as if he had been taking sips of tea, instead of his wife.

"My lord," the butler answered, taking no notice of the passionate scene he had just interrupted, "Lady Imogene wondered if my lady might have lost herself in her new surroundings. She sent me to find her. Shall I tell her that you are conducting Lady de Maine about the premises?" Chiswick maintained a calm facade, not turning a hair at the sight of the earl nuzzling his wife.

"Please tell my mother that we shall be with her shortly, Chiswick. I wish to show Lady de Maine a few of the prizes here at Pentalwyn." Again a wicked gleam shone in his gray eyes.

"Certainly, sir." The elderly butler made a leg before turning away. He stopped, then turned back. "If I may wish you and your lady happy, my lord. The rest of the staff join me in those sentiments, I'm sure." Chiswick then turned with great dignity and took himself off without a backward glance.

At first embarrassed to have been caught in what was most certainly a compromising situation, Eleanor had tried to pull away from her husband. His strong arms had held onto her, never relaxing their grasp. Finally she stopped struggling. The scene was absurd. Here was a "bride" of more than eight years being found in the impassioned embrace of her husband, whom she hardly knew, being wished happy by a stalwart butler who hadn't turned a hair upon discovering the "newlyweds" practically ready to fall on the floor in passion.

She choked back a chuckle, then pushed against Geoffrey's shoulders, struggling to free herself.

"Not yet, Eleanor. We are just beginning to come to an understanding. Don't run away from me now." A beguiling smile deepened the creases of his cheeks.

Anger flared up in her. "You take advantage of me and then have the audacity to say we are coming to an understanding? Understanding of what, my lord? You have a very limited understanding of me, if that's what you mean." She mustn't let him know how much his touch had affected her. If she could only hope that he felt some regard for her as a person, she might happily allow him to have his way with her. But to be used as a substitute for Alvinia would be too much.

"I would have said we shared the moment, my dear. Can you deny that you were as much affected by our kiss as I was? That you enjoyed our romp last night any less than I did? Don't take me for some kind of flat, wife, that I don't recognize a mutual passion."

"Let go of me, Geoffrey." Once more she pushed away from him. This time he released her. "I refuse to admit that the 'passion' was mutual. Or if it was"—a blush covered her face—"it was the product of an uncontrollable urge that women are subject to just as men are. But I refuse to give in to it. I will not be a replacement for Lady Codface!"

The earl gave a shout of laughter. "Lady Codface! How could you, Eleanor?"

"Oh dear, you weren't supposed to hear that . . ." Confused, Eleanor forgot the speech she had been about to

make. "Geoffrey! Stop laughing! Oh, this is too much."
She started to stalk away from him, only to be stopped
when he moved quickly to her side and placed an arm
about her shoulders.

"I do believe you named her rightly. She does have
the look of a fish about her, doesn't she?" He stroked
Eleanor's cheek with a gentle finger. "Now come, smile
at me. We must come to an understanding, for the benefit
of our son as well as for the ease of our lives together.
I promise I shall try not to do anything that will displease
or discomfort you. But you must promise likewise not
to push me away. There, I believe I see a touch of a
smile just about to move your lips. Give me one more
kiss, and I shall take you to my mother." He touched
her mouth softly with his, more a salutation and the
sealing of a bargain than an impassioned caress.

Mentally shrugging her shoulders, Eleanor acknowledged that Geoffrey could be irresistible. She knew she
had lost her heart to this man long ago. That she was
already married to him made the situation no better,
because he neither understood nor loved her. She could
hope that he would someday come to look at her with
love—if he hadn't yet lost the ability to love anyone.

"Come, I'll show you the jade collection and then
we'll visit Mama. Let everything slide from your mind.
It will all come right in the end, you'll see." Geoffrey
took Eleanor's hand in his and brought it to his lips,
placing a kiss in the palm. He curved her fingers over it
as though giving her something to hold. Then, once more
placing an arm around her waist, he led her from the
room.

CHAPTER FOUR

DURING THE DAYS that followed, while the earl and his countess attempted to arrive at some acceptable arrangement upon which to base their lives together, they were observed closely. Alvinia and her mother, Lady Stoneleigh, had celebrated the triumph of Alvinia's successful attachment to Geoffrey de Maine as soon as he had proposed. Their creditors had agreed to hold off dunning the women until after the wedding on the promise that the marriage settlement would more than amply take care of all due bills. Lady Stoneleigh was now beside herself with anger at the disruption of her daughter's expected wedding and was thoroughly berating her for the debacle.

"She must be gotten rid of, it's the only answer." The older woman bordered on hysteria.

"Of course she must be . . . and she will be," Alvinia answered calmly. "She comes from nowhere, without any warning, and the fool doesn't even remember marrying her, yet he is ready to accept her and her brat without any substantial proof. She could have had the lines forged or counterfeited for a few guineas, but he doesn't even question them. The fool!" She sat down at the tambour desk, accompanying her statement with a rapid tapping of her long nails against the polished furniture. "Thank goodness de Maine has never been stingy. The jewelry he's given me will be enough to hold off the wolves for a few months, and we shall have to cancel the trousseau. Trousseau, ha! *She'll* be getting all the clothes now." The irate woman turned to her mother. "Mama! Stop your moaning. We'll come about, I promise. No little chit from nowhere is going to alter *my* plans. It will take a little longer to win my goal—that is all."

"I told you you should have pushed up the wedding date. But no, you were so sure of the man that you wanted to flaunt your triumph with a wedding at St. George's in Hanover Square. Now you'll never have the *ton* at your feet. You'll hear them laughing instead! I told you— oh, my heart—I'm sure I'm going to die." The plump woman, tied tightly into her stays, languished on the sofa.

Alvinia reached for her reticule, removed a vinaigrette from its depths, and walked slowly to her mother's side to wave it beneath her nose. "Stop fainting, Mama. We have no time for such nonsense. We have to plan. Just let me think for a moment. I have the glimmer of an idea, and it begins with our taking our leave as soon as possible. But in such a way that de Maine will feel gratitude for my understanding and good wishes. Yes, it's most important that there be good feelings between us."

Lady Stoneleigh sat up, her color restored by the hope that her daughter's manner inspired. "But I should think that, if you leave the field clear to her, you'll lose every advantage. Without your presence, he is liable to forget you entirely. She *is* quite beautiful—in her own fashion, you know—and he's becoming besotted with her."

"Oh, infatuation . . . it's only for the moment. She's new to him, but what difference? He was never dissatisfied with *me*. He won't forget *me* so quickly. It's just unfortunate that he wasn't more enamored of me. I don't think he has it in him to love any woman and so, as long as he doesn't love *her,* I shall win him back."

Alvinia stepped to the bedroom doorway and called

out to her abigail. "Becket! We leave tomorrow. Start packing."

"Oh, Alvinia, I don't want to go back. The tradesmen'll be at the door before the knocker is up," her mother wailed. "Damn that woman. How could he have married so long ago and never remembered it?" Her eyes squeezed shut in thought. "It must have been about the time you married Coddington. You never should have jilted him, you foolish girl."

"*I* didn't want to marry Coddington, Mama. It was you and my father who thought his fortune so great. Pity you didn't know his pockets were almost to let and that there was barely enough to keep us above water. What a joke! *He* thought *me* an heiress, and we thought him rich as Croesus. Everything that might have been turned to cash was entailed upon his heir. What good did that do us, I ask you? You were a foolish woman then, and you're a foolish woman now. But this time *I'll* do the planning, and *you* will do the listening."

"You wanted the title and the money, my dear, so don't try your tales on me! I'm your mother and know the truth of the matter."

"If not for you, I wouldn't be in this fix right now," Alvinia insisted. "I would have accepted *carte blanche* from de Maine and had my lovely house, my carriage and four, and jewels and money—lots of money. He would have taken care of everything, and his wife's arrival would have had no meaning."

"Alvinia! How can you say that? You thankless gel! After I did everything for you . . ." Lady Stoneleigh held a wisp of lawn to her eyes, ready to dry unshed tears.

"Oh, do be quiet, Mama. This is me—Alvinia—you're speaking to. Stop telling me what's wrong and let's think of what to do to bring about that woman's downfall. To start off, you will have to excuse our abrupt departure on the pretext that an old disorder is bothering you and you must see your doctor."

"But Lady Imogene is likely to insist that I see hers."

"It won't matter. You will tell her that you have faith in no one but Dr. Bellows. Yes, that's the way to begin. Send Becket to find her ladyship and give her your sad tale. I shall tell de Maine before we meet for dinner. Becket, see that my violet gown with the silver embroidery is set out for this evening."

Alvinia seated herself once more at the desk, this time removing a piece of writing paper, a quill, and a bottle of ink from the drawer. "I must write a very pretty note to Geoffrey begging his attendance. I shall be repentant for my harsh words to his wife and all charm and tenderness about my feelings for him. I shall wish him happy, expressing with sighs my sadness at having our future thwarted. Then I shall smile bravely and hope that the unkind words his wife had to say about him and his family were only passing comments of no moment. With a gentle kiss placed chastely upon his cheek, I shall hope that we can always be friends."

A cynical grimace curved Alvinia's pouting mouth as she continued, "That should make him feel like a raw recruit. He will have expected weeping and wailing, I'm sure, and will be only too desirous of agreeing because he will see I'm pluck to the backbone. Ummm . . . that's the way of it. The passing comment about dear Eleanor will not fall on barren ground. It will produce a crop later, if not at once.

"And then Mama," Alvinia continued, "we shall go to London and prepare for the arrival of the Earl and Countess de Maine. They are sure to be in residence for the season to introduce the new countess to the *ton*. Oh, yes, we'll see that she's properly introduced."

Lady Stoneleigh gave a neigh of laughter. "My dear, if you were not my daughter, you would positively frighten me!"

*   *   *

Lady Coddington and her mother continued to refine their plans without being aware that, at the same time, Lady Imogene and Mrs. Ogden were finding themselves in agreement about the possible harm that the earl's jilted fiancée might bring to Eleanor.

"Of course it would be to the advantage of the marriage if we could gently—very gently, mind you," Mrs. Ogden was saying to Lady Imogene, "encourage your son and my dear Eleanor to come to a greater degree of sentiment. Did you sense any kind of . . . of . . . harmonious inclination between them, my lady?"

"I do believe that they are more attracted to each other than they will admit to themselves," the earl's mother responded. "Despite Geoffrey's sometimes aloof manner, he is at heart a most warm and sentimental fellow. As a matter of fact, Mrs. Ogden, I—"

"Oh, please, do call me Lucretia. I feel that we shall become very good friends."

"Certainly. Thank you, Lucretia, and you must call me Immy. Only my dearest friend called me that, and I would love to hear it again. Well," Lady Imogene went on, "to the business at hand. What was I saying? Oh, yes, Geoffrey. He really is the best of sons. Even though I'm his mother, I feel I may say that without prejudice. It would have broken my heart to have seen him enter into a marriage of convenience with *that woman*. Which is really all it would have been, you know. He certainly deserves better."

"To be sure," Mrs. Ogden agreed, "to be sure. I am positive he will find a loving wife in Eleanor. I know that she was greatly attached to him when she first came to us. Despite her subsequent protestations that she held him in complete disgust, I am convinced that she harbors a *tendresse* for him. One usually does for the man who is one's first lover. And in this case one's only lover and the father of the child she adores."

"I do agree with you, my dear Lucretia. Would you like another cup of tea?" Lady Imogene lifted the Spode teapot, ready to refill the thin porcelain cups. At Mrs. Ogden's nod, she proceeded to pour and add sugar and cream, then handed her guest the filled cup. "Now, if only we can make these two aware of their own feelings...for I am sure Geoffrey has taken a great fancy to Eleanor. What a wonderful thing that they are already married. Half the battle is won!" A trill of delighted laughter rose in the air. "I'll tell you what I think we should do. Encourage them to remain here for a few weeks so that the three of them—Phillip, Eleanor and Geoffrey—can become more easy in each other's presence. Then we shall go to London. I am already planning a gala of the first order to introduce my daughter-in-law to society. The beginning of May should be a good time, which will give them all of spring, the loveliest time of the year, to *find* each other.

"We mustn't let them know that we are providing the opportunities for them to be together," Lady Imogene continued. "Geoffrey will balk if he thinks he's being managed. He's a trifle pigheaded, one must admit, son or not!"

"My dear Immy, one could almost say the same of Eleanor. Usually a most tractable woman, vastly accommodating, never disobliging. But every once in a while something will strike her the wrong way, and then it's flat-out disaster to try to convince her the road's taken a twist in the opposite direction from which it should go. When that happens, it's no good trying anything. She just has to come to her own turnaround. I must admit it doesn't happen very often, thank goodness, but when it does..." The good lady sighed.

"We shall have to make certain that we put nothing in the way to cause any such behavior. The question is, how shall we convince Alvinia to leave the scene?" Lady Imogene's brow wrinkled in thought. "It would be just like her to stay and stay out of sheer obstreperousness."

A tap on the door interrupted their ruminations.

"Come," Lady Imogene called.

"My lady." Lady Stoneleigh's maid, Becket, entered the room. "Lady Stoneleigh sent me to ask that you forgive her, but a recurrent disorder has forced her to take to her bed, and she will not be able to join you for dinner tonight. She also expressed her regrets that she must leave Pentalwyn first thing tomorrow morning. She wishes to consult with her doctor as soon as possible."

"Oh, dear, the poor soul," exclaimed Lady Imogene. "I shall send for my medical man. She shouldn't wait until she gets to London if she is feeling so low."

"Thank you, my lady, but my mistress feels that only her doctor will be able to help her. If you could send ahead to the posting houses so that arrangements are made for her arrival at each one, it would be greatly appreciated. My lady asked me to express her deepest gratitude for your help." Upon receiving Lady Imogene's acquiescence, Becket turned to leave the room then turned back to add, "Lady Coddington will accompany her mother. She also expressed her appreciation, my lady, and will explain further at dinner tonight."

"Well, that takes care of one problem," Mrs. Ogden commented once Becket had closed the door behind her. "Their absence will make the whole affair much easier to handle."

"To be sure," Lady Imogene agreed, "but I can't help wondering why Alvinia is giving up the field so easily."

"My dear Immy," Mrs. Ogden started, "surely she realized that she can't have a marriage set aside to gain her objective, at least not without the husband's consent. And he didn't seem anxious to attempt any such course of action."

"Oh, I have no doubt that she would have accepted

carte blanche had Geoffrey offered it, but for that she would have stayed. No, I have a feeling about this, Lucretia. I'm afraid that we will hear further from that woman." Lady Imogene's faded blue eyes were worried. "I wonder if we might suggest another wedding ceremony, just as a renewal of the wedding vows, so to speak. Not that I think they're really necessary, you understand, but just in case . . ."

"What a lovely idea! But how shall we go about convincing our loved ones that they should wed again?" Mrs. Ogden hitched her voluminous skirts around as she moved closer to Lady Imogene and lowered her voice. "Do you suppose we could talk them into it? And would they need another license? They might both take fright from the idea and refuse as a matter of principle."

Lady Imogene considered deeply for some moments. "Now this isn't something that we must positively do, but just suppose the vicar who performed the marriage should, by some strange quirk of fate, happen to be in London at the same time that we make our stay there. And just suppose that some friend of ours should happen to have made his acquaintance in the interim, and, being familiar with our family, would have heard the strange tale of the forgotten bride and, on hearing the name of the vicar, recollects that he is the very one who performed the ceremony in the first place. And then, just suppose that our friend decides to introduce the vicar to me! And imagine how delighted I shall be at the thought of seeing my son and daughter-in-law recreate the ceremony, this time with suitable pomp and circumstance, for my sole pleasure. And of course we would invite a few friends and relatives to act as witnesses, as it were." Lady Imogene clapped her hands at the delightful picture she had just painted. "You see, it is a mere bagatelle to arrange, is it not, Lucretia?"

"My dear Immy, a brilliant invention. But don't you

think it relies on too many coincidences? Might your little script arouse some suspicions in certain quarters?"

"Oh, pooh! I never would have taken you for a spoil-sport, Lucretia. I assure you, it will be arranged quite easily. In fact, if you can get the name of the vicar for me and the place where he was located, I shall write to a very dear friend, a former colonel in His Majesty's Fourth, who travels around a great deal. He would be delighted to help us in this little endeavor.

"Which reminds me, I have quite forgotten to write to my daughter to inform her that I am a grandmother. Madeline will undoubtedly be shocked."

"Will you have her come here or go directly to London to wait upon you there?"

"No need for her to go anywhere at present, but as soon as we get to London, I'll have her join us. Although I can't wait for her to meet Pip. I know she'll love him. Where is he, do you suppose?"

"The last I saw of him, he and Linnet were playing tag on the south lawn. They had just finished a game of hide-and-seek in the topiary garden, and I'll tell you it was wonderful to watch."

Someone else was enjoying the sight of the slim, dark-haired woman chasing after the small, laughing boy. Geoffrey stood at the window of the morning room, thinking that it had been years since he had forgotten his dignity enough to take part in such an innocent game. He pushed open the french door and walked onto the terrace, drawn to his son and wife, wanting to join them at their play, but too aware of his own consequence to release his inhibitions.

As she twisted away from Pip's outstretched hands, Eleanor caught sight of the tall figure watching from the distance. Her step faltered momentarily as she sensed the steel-gray eyes on her. Pip's laughter faded away to be replaced by the amorous murmur of Geoffrey's voice when he held her in his arms, enclosed by the curtains of the great tester bed.

Despite the coolness between them during the days, the nights were warm with their passion. Once he put his hand on her, she was unable to refuse him. Time after time, her body rose to meet his, relishing the quickened pulses, the flames of excitement, the rapture of adoration. Repeatedly she had found herself in his arms, returning his caresses.

Lost in her memories, Eleanor failed to see a shallow depression in the lawn and took a misstep. Her foot came down too hard and she fell, skirts flaring, arms flung out in an attempt to gain her balance. Pip, who was following closely behind her, tripped over her leg and tumbled across her, saving himself from harm by landing on her body.

Instinctively Eleanor threw her arms around Pip and held him close, too winded to move. Finally, chuckling at the mishap, she asked if he were hurt. He squeezed his arms around her neck and assured her that he had suffered no damage, then asked if she were all of a piece. Their concern for each other was so great that they were unaware of Geoffrey's approach.

"Eleanor, Phillip, are you all right?" Concern sounded in the harsh voice. "What are you laughing at? Pip, help your mother to stand. Is your foot hurt? I saw you tumble and was afraid you might have twisted your ankle . . . or worse."

As he waited for an answer, his eyes were held captive by the bright laughter on the faces of his wife and son. It was the first time he had seen Eleanor without her habitual cloak of daytime decorum. Her hazel eyes shone, and an elusive dimple twinkled in her cheek. Her lips were spread in a smile that enfolded him in her happiness. Without further thought, he bent down and lifted her into his arms, prepared to carry her back to the terrace where she would be able to sit down.

"Geoffrey, what are you doing? Put me down!" Eleanor commanded, wishing only to be held in her husband's strong arms. "Whatever will anyone think if they see you carrying me like this?"

"Are you going to carry Mama all the way to the bench, Papa?" Pip began to skip along beside his father. "I guess she wouldn't be too heavy for you. I knew you were strong. I even bet Jed Doakes that you could level the champion if you was to try."

"Thank you, Pip, but I don't think I shall try. Carrying your mother is about as much as I care to do today," Geoffrey answered Pip absently, concentrating on Eleanor's face, enjoying the warmth of her body in his arms.

Eleanor hid her eyes as a delicate flush rose over her cheekbones. I *am* his wife, she told herself as she put her arms around his neck, relishing the strength of the hard muscles that held her. She allowed her head to rest against his shoulder, telling herself that there was really nothing wrong in such an act. After all, she might be feeling a little faint from her fall . . . and in need of support. Ripples of sensation moved through her at his touch. His fingertips rested against the swell of her breast, creating a desire in her that shocked her in its intensity. As her nipples began to harden with passion, she struggled against her captivity, afraid that Geoffrey would become aware of her arousal.

"Put me down, Geoffrey—immediately," she insisted.

"Why? Don't you find it pleasant to have a willing slave to carry you about?" Laughter crinkled the corners of his gray eyes. "What do you think, son? Shouldn't the lady be grateful for the service?"

Without waiting for Pip's answer, Geoffrey continued walking, not stopping until he had mounted the shallow steps to the terrace. He paused and captured her lips in a brief, sweet kiss that left her feeling as though her bones had melted.

"Geoffrey...I..."

"Don't speak." He placed her gently on the stone bench, sliding his hands along her arms before releasing her completely. "We'll talk tonight, Eleanor."

"I..." Soft with desire, Eleanor was unable to answer and merely nodded in reply.

From a window above the terrace a pair of cold blue eyes watched the interplay between the two adults below, assessing their emotions. A hot thread of hatred spread through Alvinia. She would have to put her plan in motion before the intruder had won her objective. No woman alive was going to keep Geoffrey de Maine from being hers, Alvinia vowed. No woman alive!

CHAPTER FIVE

WITH THE DEPARTURE of Lady Coddington, the atmosphere at Pentalwyn became less hostile. Lady Imogene and Mrs. Ogden observed the earl and his countess. At times the two ladies were almost sure that husband and wife had reached an agreeable conclusion to their long separation, but just as the ladies were ready to relax their vigilance, they would see the earl turn cold in his response to Eleanor. In the same way, the softness in Eleanor's eyes when she looked at Geoffrey would often harden, as if she recalled his past.

By the beginning of April, some four weeks after Eleanor and Pip had joined the family at Pentalwyn, Lady Imogene was ready to sweep up her errant son and daughter-in-law and carry them off to London, hoping that a change of scene would have a more salubrious effect upon the marriage. When she announced her plan to Eleanor, the young woman begged for a delay until Phillip should be more at ease with the new tutor who had just taken up residence at the Hall. Lady Imogene agreed to wait. The family would still arrive in London in time for the ball in early May that would honor her son and his bride. It was scheduled to be the opening festivity of the season.

"My dear, I want everyone to meet my exceptional daughter-in-law. This will be a fete to outdo all others. I've already notified my man of business that the ballroom of Hellistone House is to be repainted. I discussed the matter with dear Lucretia, and we decided upon a pale pink picked out with gold and white on the moldings and around the windows. I've ordered pink and white roses from our florists and yards of ribbons to match. I even thought we might let loose a flock of white doves at midnight—to symbolize your love." Lady Imogene sighed at the delightful picture she imagined. "Can you think of anything more . . . more . . ."

"Dizzying?" Eleanor supplied. "Can't you see the dozens of doves leaving little messages all over the guests? And then landing in the elaborate coiffures to nestle amidst the flowers and jewels they'll find there?" As she enlarged upon the event Eleanor began to giggle, finding her description droll in the extreme.

"Darling child, I'm simply trying to design a party that will do you justice." Lady Imogene tried to look serious, but Eleanor's suggestions soon had her laughing. "Oh, very well. Perhaps doves would be a bit extreme. But do you like the color scheme? It would suit your dark hair so well."

"Does Geoffrey know about your plans?" The two women were alone in Lady Imogene's parlor. "Has he agreed to all this?"

"I don't need Geoffrey's approval for my entertainments. He will not be footing the bills for this. This comes from my own resources," Lady Imogene answered indignantly.

"Dear Belle-mère, you haven't answered my question. I didn't ask about the expenses. I wish to know if my husband wishes me to have such a . . . a . . . *bold* introduction to the *ton*."

"I saw no reason to burden him with the idea." Lady Imogene refused to meet Eleanor's eyes.

"You are still not answering my question, Belle-mère. Are you sure he'll even honor us with his presence?"

"Of course he'll be there! He has too much pride to

slight his family in such a way. Enough of worrying! We leave for London in two weeks. We'll have time for a leisurely trip—I must tell you I'm not the best of travelers. When we arrive, there will be so many things we will have to arrange for the ball. I vow, I'm quite excited by the thought. I love the quiet life here in Cornwall, but I do look forward to London." Lady Imogene pondered on the joys of Town, then continued. "Now, help me make a list of the things we absolutely *must* have in the way of gowns. I think you will need at least three walking dresses and a new mantua and a . . ."

Eleanor protested that her wardrobe was quite extensive and needed only a few additions to prepare her for the coming season, but Lady Imogene insisted that it was her daughter-in-law's duty to become known as the best-dressed woman in London. She had already invited Madame Vouillard, the foremost couturiere in England, to Pentalwyn. The woman had arrived that very day accompanied by ten seamstresses, a coach full of yard goods newly imported from France and Italy, forms for hats, lengths of sheerest cashmere, and lace for shawls and trimmings, a bootmaker with his leathers, and boxes of feathers, buttons, and assorted oddments necessary to complete the most lavish clothes.

"Tomorrow morning we shall start the fittings, and you may choose some patterns from the dress dolls that Madame brought with her. I particularly want you to have something ravishing for the ball. Geoffrey must have the pink sapphires cleaned so that you can wear them that night." Lady Imogene was like a general marshaling her forces.

"Whatever you say, dearest." Eleanor could only acquiesce in the face of a *force majeure*. "But I have my own jewels. There's no need for Geoffrey—"

"There's no need for me to what?" Geoffrey's entrance into the room had gone unnoticed. His tall form looked especially striking in buff-colored buckskins and a russet jacket that was almost the same color as his hair as he lounged against the edge of the doorway. Eleanor drew a deep breath, feeling a physical response to his lean grace, remembering the feel of his hard body against hers.

"Oh, Geoffrey, I'm so glad you came in. I wished to remind you to have the Hellistone jewels taken from the safe and cleaned. Eleanor will be needing a few of the pieces, especially the sapphires." Lady Imogene turned her cheek towards her son, inviting his salutation. "She has some hen-brained notion that she needn't wear them."

"But it's part of the perquisites of being a bride of the Hellistones." Geoffrey's words sounded sarcastic. "And what woman would the gems grace more beautifully than my wife?"

"I had thought to save you the bother of having them cleaned." Eleanor lifted her chin. "I have some quite beautiful jewels left me by Miss Shappley."

"Ah, yes, the ubiquitous Miss Shappley. How kind of her to have taken such good care of you. And Phillip, of course."

Geoffrey's attitude astonished his listeners as well as himself. He had been fighting the strengthening pull of Eleanor's charm and beauty. Never before had a woman so entwined herself into his being, creating a dependency upon her in this way. He fought her power over him, not ready yet to admit that he loved her. He also resented her independence. That she came to him without needing his support irked him, making him feel an irrational anger at both Eleanor and her benefactress, Miss Shappley. Yet there were times when he melted towards his wife. His senses became inflamed in her presence, and he found himself constantly fighting a need to carry her off to some private place where they could be alone.

Lady Imogene was shocked at the bitterness in her son's voice. "Geoffrey! Show a little respect for the mem-

ory of that wonderful woman. If not for her care of
Eleanor, we might never have had the delight of having
her with us... and our dear little Pip. We owe her a
great debt that can never be repaid. I don't wish to hear
any more such remarks from you."

"Your pardon, ma'am. It was *farouche* of me to speak
so. Of course the jewelry will be made ready for my
wife. In fact, I have decided to leave for London in the
morning." Geoffrey's news surprised the women no less
than it surprised him. He made his decision to leave
without thought, knowing only that it was dangerous to
remain in Eleanor's company. "My man is packing my
bags at this moment. Do you have any commissions for
me that will make your arrival there any easier?"

"Isn't your decision rather sudden, my lord?" Eleanor
asked, unable to look at Geoffrey lest the hurt show in
her eyes. "I thought you were to accompany us on our
trip."

"I had thought to originally, but certain unexpected
business has been brought to my attention." He moved
his hand in a casual gesture as though to indicate that
his interest in her company was not so all consuming as
to keep him by her side. "You and Mama will be safe
enough. There will be several outriders and two wagons,
as well as your coach and the coach with the servants.
No need for me to delay just to accompany you."

"You surprise me, son," said Lady Imogene. "What
can be so urgent that you have to leave?" Lady Imogene
was disturbed by the coolness between husband and wife.
She had seen an occasional indication that all was not as
she hoped it to be, but had attributed the slight chill to
a small marital spat. However, this was different. She
wondered what had happened to cause the rift.

"I don't think the exact reason for my going to London
would interest you, dear Mama. Suffice it to say I have
need of my friends and they of me." Geoffrey rose from

the sofa. "I beg you to excuse me. So much to do. Must give instructions to the bailiff." Just as abruptly as he had appeared, he left the room.

Eleanor was bewildered by Geoffrey's latest turn of manners. She had thought he was coming to return her regard. At night he had shown an ardor that gave her pleasure beyond her wildest dreams. But his interest in her as a person was as variable as the weather; he was content with her on fine days and coldly aloof on stormy days. She almost wished she had never come to Pentalwyn, never read the announcement of his impending marriage to Alvinia, never fallen in love with him.

Eleanor had no idea that his changing disposition was a result of his growing love for her. He found himself enjoying her presence, her laughter, her bright intelligence, and her passionate response to his lovemaking. She was everything he could want in a woman, and he wanted none and all of her at once. His increasing dependence upon her company, his need for the stimulating interchanges between them, and his wish for the warmth of her affection all began to frighten him.

Long years before, he had sworn that he would never love a woman as he had loved Alvinia. Instead of happiness, his love had brought only disillusionment and pain. Now that he was once more in love—this time with his own wife—he fought his feelings and sought his freedom. He told himself he didn't want to be tied to any one woman.

To prove to himself that he had the liberty he thought he wished for, he would withhold his favors from Eleanor periodically. Now, as though to underline his exemption from the bonds of matrimony, he had decided to spend two weeks in London playing at being the bachelor. He had already penned a note to a former light-of-love, instructing her that he was desirous of her company.

"Well!" Lady Imogene exclaimed. "I must say that there are times when I simply do *not* understand my son.

Have you quarreled Eleanor?" she asked as gently as she could.

"No, Belle-mère, there's been nothing like that between us." Eleanor gazed into the fire. "I must confess that I find my husband a difficult man to understand. Every time I think we are getting on well, he does something that gives me the impression that I have displeased him mightily. I don't know. Perhaps we should abandon the plan to go up to London."

"Abandon! Never! We are going to London, and *you* are going to become *le dernier cri*, the rage of the *ton*, the...the..." Lady Imogene's emotion proved an impediment to her descriptive abilities. "Never mind. If he is going to ignore us, *we* shall ignore him. If he weren't my son, I'd ring a peal over his head that would give him a migraine to last a month!"

A broad smile lit Eleanor's face. It was impossible to remain gloomy in the face of Lady Imogene's enthusiasm. "Very well, Mama, whatever you say. I hope you can contain your choler long enough to see us packed and on our way."

Her eyes began to dance at the thought that her dignified husband might be riding for a fall at her hands. Not that she wished to see him hurt. But to be able to prick his pride might serve as a satisfactory vengeance for the sorrow he had caused her. If her mama-in-law wished her to be the newest incomparable in the coming season, she would do her best to give that lady her wish. With the arts that Mrs. Ogden and Miss Shappley had taught her, she had no qualms as to her ability to conduct herself as to the manor born. Yes, it should prove very satisfying to confound her *confounded* mate.

CHAPTER SIX

SOME THREE-AND-A-HALF weeks later a magnificent coach drawn by six matched grays pulled into the courtyard of Hellistone House just off Grosvenor Square in London. It was followed by several other vehicles carrying servants, boxes, trunks, and assorted furniture that Lady Imogene needed with her for her comfort. A small Pekinese dog yapped at the bustle, further adding to the excitement surrounding the arrival.

Lady Imogene, Mrs. Ogden, and Eleanor straightened their bonnets and skirts before allowing the smiling butler to help them from the coach.

"Parkins, thank you," said the dowager countess to the stalwart servant who handed her down from the plush carriage. "Is my son at home?"

"No, my lady, we haven't had the pleasure of the earl's presence these past three days." He offered his help to the other two ladies.

"Humph, I expected better of him," the old countess exclaimed vexatiously. "Eleanor, we have a great deal to do before this evening. Lucretia, will you help the dear girl choose a gown for dinner? I know we have a great deal of mail to go through, and I'm sure there are more invitations and calling cards than we'll need to keep busy the rest of the week." She issued a string of instructions as she walked up the steps of the portico leading into the gracious mansion.

"Wouldn't you rather rest this evening, Belle-mère? You must be exhausted from the traveling today." Eleanor followed her closely into the spacious entry foyer and breathed a sigh of appreciation at the beauty of the decor.

The broad black-and-white marble floor was outlined with strips of inlaid brass that repeated the color of the gold-leaf dado. Fluted Doric pilasters supporting classic architraves created the settings for the various doors that led from the foyer into several of the ground-floor rooms. At the far end of the entry, a double-winged staircase rose to the second floor and thence upward to the skylight of delicate spiderweb ironwork that supported the clear glass. A pair of tables from Mr. Sheraton's workrooms faced each other on opposite walls and were flanked by chairs covered in pale straw-colored silk that matched the walls. Black urns of ancient Greek origin were fitted into niches in the walls, complementing the dark tone of the floor, and a magnificent candelabra of bronze and crystal that matched several wall sconces hung in the center.

Despite the simplicity of the design, the entrance intimated that the rest of the house would be opulent but tasteful.

"Come along, my dear," Lady Imogene commanded. "Don't gawk. You'll have a chance to see everything before long. Parkins, I wish Mrs. Ogden to be settled in the blue suite next to mine. We'll have much planning to do, so we'd best be near one another. Lady de Maine is to be in the master suite. I hope it's been prepared?"

"Of course, my lady. The master instructed us." The butler looked down his long nose. "If you would come into the drawing room, you need not be disturbed by the servants' preparations."

The ladies gratefully entered the beautiful chamber with its graceful Chippendale furniture, lush French carpets, and exquisite appointments. Although Pentalwyn was beautiful, nothing there equaled the sophisticated elegance of this room, which was as comfortable as it was magnificent.

With a sigh that was almost a groan, Mrs. Ogden sat down on one of the three sofas and unfastened the ties of her hat. She placed it on the seat beside her. "I think I shall be jouncing around for the next several weeks. As well sprung as your coach is, Immy, riding in it is not as soothing to my old bones as sitting on this piece of furniture."

"I know, my dear, it's been a long trip," Lady Imogene agreed. "But now we can settle in for a good, long stay, and you need not ride in a carriage at all if you don't wish to." Lady Imogene settled herself on a comfortable armchair next to Mrs. Ogden. "Find a seat, Linnet. Parkins ordered tea for us, unless you'd rather have ratafia or a glass of negus?"

"No, tea will be fine. As soon as we finish, though, I would like to rest for a while. Why do you want Lucretia to help me choose a gown for tonight?"

"I thought I told you. We are going to an intimate gathering of some two hundred guests at the Duchess of Mainfort's. She's having a musicale—that Italian soprano. What's her name? Well, it doesn't really matter what her name is, for she's fat as a pig and will be no worry to anyone. Where was I? Oh, yes, since it's imperative that you be seen by the *haut monde* as soon as possible, we shall attend. I think you should wear the apricot gauze with the gold underskirt. You look very well in it and will make a good impression."

Mrs. Ogden straightened her shawl, then picked up the top envelope from the pile of letters and notes on the table. "Do you want to start going through these now while we wait for tea? We'll have to choose very carefully the entertainments that we wish to go to." She gave a speaking glance to Lady Imogene, letting one eyelid droop in a warning wink.

Eleanor was not aware of *all* the plans the two companions had made for her. Some were devious to an extreme. Lady Imogene had decided that her son needed to be shocked out of his complacent attitude towards his lovely wife. To effect that, she and Mrs. Ogden planned to encourage Eleanor to attach one or two *cicisbeos*. It was not uncommon for a married lady to have several admirers who stood as her escorts when her husband was unavailable. In some cases, of course, the privileges went beyond mere platonic friendship, but such liaisons were not frowned upon as long as the participants were not *blatant* in the way they conducted their affairs. Not that they expected Eleanor to carry matters to such an end.

As Mrs. Ogden expressed it, the problem would be that Linnet was so honest and forthright she would hardly undertake an *affaire de coeur* while married. She had also admitted that she was too deeply in love with Geoffrey to even wish for the attention of another man. The two conspirators had made suggestions to each other about ways in which they could coerce their unhappy Eleanor into playing the role that they felt would bring her ultimate happiness, but thus far they had come up with no sensible plan.

"Is it really necessary for us to go out this evening?" Eleanor asked plaintively. "I'm really so tired."

"Of course it's necessary," Lady Imogene replied. "I promised Cordelia that we'd make an appearance. She's a very old and dear friend of mine, and I owe it to her to allow her to be the first hostess to bring you to the attention of our friends." Lady Imogene acknowledged the arrival of a retinue of servants carrying trays filled with cups and saucers, teapots, chocolate pots, pitchers, plates of cream cakes, and small hot savories. "You'll feel much better once you've had a bit of food and an hour's rest. Lucretia, would you do me the honor of pouring? No milk in my tea. Oh, by the by, dear child, I understand that very nice friend of Geoffrey's, Jeremy

Broadbent, is to be present this evening. Charming boy. And so pleasant...so accommodating. I wrote inviting him to attend us at dinner tomorrow evening. He replied immediately. Most gratifying. Said he'd not been able to get you out of his mind since he'd met you at Pentalwyn. Do you remember him?"

"Yes, he was very...polite. But I only spoke with him a few moments the day I arrived at the Hall. He, as well as the rest of the guests—except Alvinia—left Pentalwyn the following day, and I had no further opportunity to speak with any of them." Eleanor sipped the hot liquid, letting its warmth comfort her and melt the coldness she had felt since finding out that the earl had not been present for the past few days.

What was he up to, to have ignored her for such a long time? If only she could love him less. If only she could resist him when he came to her room at night. But, once he touched her, she was lost. The pangs of desire that she felt at the thought of his hands and lips on her body, at the remembrance of his fierce lovemaking, were as strong as if they were pangs of pain. Why couldn't she look upon him with the same coldness with which he seemed to regard her? Life would be so much less complicated.

"Well," Lady Imogene began again, "do you think the apricot gown will do? Really, my dear, you must concentrate. You must take your place in Society. I'm sure you wish to do so with style and *élan,* and there's no one more qualified than I, even though I say so myself, to help you do so. I was a leader of the *ton* when I was younger. I daresay I still have a deal of influence."

"I'm sure you do, Belle-mère. You have no need to tell me you were a very gorgon of society at one time. Why, you have me absolutely quaking at the thought of your anger should I not go along with your wishes." Eleanor gave a realistic shudder, then leaned back with a weary sigh. "Have no fear, I shall do exactly as you recommend. I wish only that you and—and—Geoffrey will be proud of me."

"Oh, piffle!" Mrs. Ogden interrupted. "Just be proud of yourself, girl. Your words lead one to believe you think too little of yourself. What happened to the young woman I've known for eight years who was so full of pluck and determination? You're here to meet people and to enjoy yourself. If Geoffrey takes a part in everything, fine. If not, so much the worse for him."

"That's right." Lady Imogene nodded in agreement. "If my son is so *stoopid* as to ignore the treasure in his own home, then I wash my hands of him!"

Eleanor eyed her two champions, who looked like major-generals on a campaign. She began to laugh helplessly at the sight of them. "Very well. I promise to love every minute of my debut. I shall learn everything you have to teach me, accept every invitation, acknowledge every acquaintance, and lead every gathering."

"With a cordial manner, Eleanor," her mother-in-law instructed, "but not one so forward as to call for too much freedom from the gentlemen."

"Really, Immy, as if Linnet would behave boldly in any case!" Mrs. Ogden fired at Lady Imogene. "She's too much the lady."

"You're right, Lucretia. Beg your pardon, Eleanor. Now, go along and have your rest. I'll send Bennett to help you dress. We'll dine at half-after-six and leave for the duchess's at eight. Be sure to look your prettiest tonight. It's most important."

It was just past eight o'clock that evening when the three ladies climbed into the carriage to be driven to the musicale. Each looked superb in her own way. Mrs. Ogden was once more attired in her layers of material, this time in dark brown with a pale apple-green turban that carried a single egret feather attached by a huge tourmaline cabochon.

Lady Imogene was the total *grande dame* in an aubergine velvet gown with a magnificent amethyst and diamond tiara, necklace, bracelet, and stomacher. She carried a chicken-skin fan painted by the renowned Swiss artist, Angelica Kauffman.

As magnificent as the two older women looked, Eleanor was the embodiment of everyone's vision of a princess. Her dark, cloud-soft locks were piled into a mass of curls surrounded by a coronet of gold wire shaped into vines. Each vine leaf was made up of peridots the exact color of spring growth. Interspersed among the leaves were tiny flowers of freshwater pearls and diamonds. The fragile masterpiece trembled at every breath, creating a shimmering halo.

Eleanor's apricot gauze dress was itself a work of art. A sheer overdress, embroidered at the high waistline and hem with the same pattern and gems of the coronet, was worn over cloth-of-gold worked in such a way that it caressed the countess's body under the fullness of the gauze. Her eyes picked up the color of the gown, glowing a deep gold with sparkling glints of green in their depths. The deep décolletage exposed shoulders of creamy white, but stopped short of revealing too great an expanse of her beautifully modeled bosom.

The drive was accomplished in short order, with the elder ladies never ceasing in their praise of Eleanor's good looks that evening. Mrs. Ogden and Lady Imogene congratulated each other silently as well, each hoping that the earl would happen in on the entertainment.

"And I hope he finds his wife surrounded by the most handsome Corinthians, at least two Top-of-the-Trees gallants and perhaps a royal or two," Lady Imogene prayed under her breath. "Such a fool as my son has turned out to be I never hoped to see."

About half of the two hundred guests had already arrived for the musical event when Lady de Maine was introduced to the Duchess of Mainfort.

"My dear, what a charming child," the tiny vivacious lady said to Lady Imogene. "I had not thought her to be quite such a *beauty*. Word has it that . . . Oh dear, I . . . *Do* excuse me, Lady de Maine. There are other guests I simply *must* greet. Shall we chat later?" As quickly as she could, the Duchess handed her guests on to the majordomo to be conducted to their seats.

"I see someone's been at work, spreading tales." Mrs. Ogden looked knowingly at Lady Imogene. "And I'm willing to wager my next quarter that it was a blond, blue-eyed nasty piece of goods. You were right to insist that we appear tonight, Immy. At the very least this should put paid to some of *that woman's* nonsense."

"Quite right, Lucretia, quite right. Oh good, we're seated just in back of Jeremy." Lady Imogene pulled Eleanor with her as she moved along the row of gilded chairs, calling a greeting to Mr. Broadbent. "Oh, Jeremy, I *am* glad to see you. Here, why don't you change seats with me so that you can talk with Eleanor during the betweens. I've been wanting a word with Lady Danwell, and it's so convenient that she's seated next to you." With the aplomb of a general, Lady Imogene reorganized the seating to suit herself. "There, that's so much better now, isn't it?" Then, ignoring the subjects of her manipulation, she proceeded to involve herself in a softly spoken conversation with the lady she professed herself so eager to speak to.

"Somewhat managerial, wouldn't you say?" Glints of humor danced in Jeremy's kind brown eyes.

"In the kindest way, of course, Mr. Broadbent," Eleanor replied. "I hope she hasn't inadvertently disturbed any arrangements you may have made."

"Of course not, my lady. I had been hoping to have a chance to become more acquainted with you." Jeremy swept his coattails out of the way as he took his seat. "How long do you intend to stay in London?"

"I'm not perfectly sure. Lady Imogene is determined

that I make my mark this season. I only hope my success is as great as she looks for." A perfect creamy shoulder shrugged slightly. "I would have been happier to remain at Pentalwyn, but she has some bee in her bonnet..."

"For as long as I've been privileged to know Lady Imogene, she has had some cause for which she has taken up the cudgels. Be glad that she has involved you in your come-out and not some great scheme to circumvent the government from running the country!"

"Oh, no! She would not be so—" Eleanor glanced at her mother-in-law, who was deep in conversation with her friend, her auburn head nodding at something Lady Danwell was saying. "You are funning, sir, and that is quite unfair of you. You must not tease me until I have come to know your sense of humor better. I might take you seriously and then what would happen? All sorts of terrible things!"

"No, never terrible things." Jeremy replied jocularly. "My dear friend Geoffrey would never allow that. He will protect me, as always." Jeremy fell silent as he became aware of Eleanor's stillness. Her laughter had been wiped away, and her eyes were frosty. "Have I said something to annoy you, my lady?" he asked. "I beg your pardon if..."

"No need to beg my pardon, sir. 'Twas a momentary twinge that sometimes besets me. Think nothing of it. Now, do tell me, have you been to the theater lately?" Eleanor managed to maintain a light chatter until the duchess appeared to announce the guest singer for the evening. Eleanor was grateful for the interruption. The last fifteen minutes had been acute torture for her. She had wanted nothing more than to rant and rave about her *wonderful* husband who thought so little of his wife that he hadn't even been present to greet her arrival after a three-week absence. And now, to have to listen to encomiums from this friend of long standing was too much to be borne.

A polite patter of applause sounded for the short, rotund woman who was taking her place next to the pianoforte. Eleanor watched disinterestedly as the woman's pudgy hands clasped under her pouter-pigeon breast. A nod was given to the accompanist, who played the introductory measures, and then the soprano opened her mouth to sing. Never would Eleanor forget the liquid beauty of the clear *bel canto* voice. She was immediately swept up by the enthralling sound. She forgot her problems and concentrated on the experience at hand. When the aria finally came to an end, she shook her head, feeling that in some way the incomparable voice had removed some of her unhappiness.

She turned to Jeremy and shared the moment silently with him. She was about to offer a comment when she saw his glance move beyond her face and a smile of welcome appear on his lips.

"Your husband has arrived, Lady de Maine. Your pardon while I greet him." Jeremy arose as he spoke. "He may have my seat for the remainder of the performance."

Eleanor turned slightly, unable to prevent herself from wishing to see her husband. She was about to nod to him when she saw his companion. Alvinia Coddington was hanging on his arm, laughing up into his smiling face.

"Don't trouble yourself, Mr. Broadbent," Eleanor replied. "He will be looking for a pair of seats, I believe. Do stay beside me." Her eyes pleaded with him. "I know so few people here—just you and Lady Imogene, as a matter of fact. I should feel deserted."

Jeremy Broadbent was not blind to the hurt on Eleanor's face. He had never known his friend to be thoughtless of his family, but it seemed that, in this case, Geoffrey was oversetting his usual behavior.

Before Jeremy could answer Eleanor, Lady Imogene stood up and noticed her son's arrival—but not his shorter companion. Excusing herself to her friend, Lady Imogene moved along the row of seats, making her way to Geoffrey's side. When she arrived there, her surprise at seeing Alvinia was noticeable only to those who knew her well. The sudden mask of reserve that wiped away her welcoming smile quickly became a mere grimace of the lips. She acknowledged Lady Coddington's presence with a stiff nod, then proceeded to ignore her as she said a few words to her son.

Eleanor watched Geoffrey's black eyebrows rise in response to something Lady Imogene said. Then his slate-gray eyes met hers across the room. She stared back at him for a moment, not acknowledging him by so much as the flicker of an eyelash. Then carefully and slowly, she turned her head as though she had not seen him. Out of the corner of her eye she saw his skin turn white and his eyes flash with anger.

"My word, Lady de Maine, you must be fearless. You've just given your husband the cut direct." Jeremy was aghast at what he had just seen. "Are you at all familiar with his temper, ma'am? I don't know whether to commend you for bravery or commiserate with your relatives at your suicidal tendencies."

"I see no reason why he should be bothered, Mr. Broadbent. He's shown as much regard for me." Eleanor suddenly realized what she had said. "Oh, dear, I'm afraid I have a temper as hot at my husband's. And it is unforgivable of me to draw you into our...mis-understanding."

"Not at all. If you promise to spend the next interlude with me so that we may continue our growing under-standing, I shall forget that you are less than the even-tempered lady I took you for." His gently chiding words and open smile of admiration helped to soothe the mixed feelings of rage and humiliation that had swept through her at the sight of Alvinia.

Once more the audience grew quiet and Madame Tor-telli's magical voice filled the room. From somewhere behind them came a piercing whisper. "And she's with Mr. Broadbent, Geoffrey. Do you think he escorted her here tonight?" Several mumbled imprecations and hissed objections warned the whisperer that some people present were more interested in Madame Tortelli's voice than hers. Silence descended once more, and Eleanor fought to recapture the tranquillity she had enjoyed earlier. It was impossible. She sat there seething at the indignity her husband had caused her.

Immediately after the conclusion of the recital, Eleanor approached Lady Imogene, hoping to escape the festivities before Geoffrey approached her.

"Belle-mère, I hope you won't mind if Mr. Broadbent escorts me home. I have a most excruciating migraine." Her golden eyes blazed with fury, giving the lie to the excuse.

"My dear, I think you would gain more by staying," Lady Imogene said gently. "The duchess is serving a collation, and it would look better if you seemed to be enjoying the gathering. You're not going to give the field to that woman, are you? Surely you're made of sterner stuff?" Lady Imogene reminded Eleanor of a jockey urging his mount on to win the race.

"Did you expect Geoffrey to arrive with *her*, Belle-mère?"

"Of course not! I wouldn't credit my son with being such a nodcock! I can't imagine what idiocy could have induced him to behave in such an incomprehensible manner." Lady Imogene patted Eleanor's arm reassuringly. "I think you should take it as a sign for you to enjoy yourself, dearest. Mr. Broadbent is willing and ready to take you in to supper, and he will introduce you to all the younger people. I believe his sister and brother-in-law are here this evening. Charming couple . . . quite up to every rig and row going, but quite without any pretension. Ah, Jeremy."

Mr. Broadbent had arrived in answer to Lady Imogene's signal. "Will you take Eleanor in to supper? She needs to meet some of the younger set, and I know you and your sister know everyone."

"My great pleasure. Do I gather that in addressing me and speaking of your daughter-in-law by our first names, you are giving us permission to do away with any further formality, Lady Imogene?"

"Of course. You are almost a member of the family so you should have the rights and privileges of a brother or cousin." Lady Imogene looked meaningfully at the young man. "I shall expect the best of you."

"But of course, ma'am." A seraphic smile met Lady Imogene's questioning look before Jeremy turned to Eleanor and offered his crooked elbow. "Shall we? Before all the lobster patties have disappeared?"

Filled with sudden determination, Eleanor decided that Geoffrey would never guess by her behavior that she was one whit hurt. With that in mind, she placed her hand on Jeremy's arm, gave him a wide smile, and allowed him to draw her away from the assembled music lovers. No one would know that her heart had been crushed by her husband's heedless behavior. No one would know that tears were standing at the edges of her eyes. No one should know that she loved her husband with a passion that startled her. No one should know, no one. Least of all him.

CHAPTER SEVEN

ELEANOR STOOD IN front of the pier-glass mirror brushing her long black hair, and pausing from time to time to contemplate some scene beyond her vision. Her filmy ecru *robe de nuit* barely concealed her pale body. The long, loose, lace-edged sleeves fell back from her raised arms, revealing their sensuous movements as the hair-brush slowly stroked her long tresses. She was an unconsciously seductive sight to her husband as he paused in the connecting door between their bedrooms.

Unaware of his presence, she continued to prepare for bed, dreaming of a perfect amity between them that was her deepest wish. He waited for her to notice his presence. He had already changed from his evening dress into a Chinese mandarin's robe of black silk with dragons and chrysanthemums embroidered on the back and side panels. The costume lent him an air of savagery that was usually not part of his makeup. His black eyebrows, in such contrast to his auburn hair, were twisted in a frown as he studied his wife.

He was furious. That she had dared to flirt with his best friend after cutting him without even a nod of greeting aroused his ire to a degree that was almost uncontrollable. How dare she treat him so in front of people who knew him! His hands clenched into fists at the thought of the ridicule that might be turned against him because of her actions this evening.

His abrupt movement as he brought his hands together caught Eleanor's attention. She whirled around, growing pale at the sight of him.

"What are you doing in here?" Her dark-fringed, amber eyes opened wide in apprehension. She knew her behavior that evening had been unforgivable, but she had had just cause. "Could you not have knocked before entering?" She struggled to keep her voice from trembling.

"My dear wife, I haven't greeted you properly after our long separation. It was too bad that you didn't see me when I arrived at the musicale this evening. Had you given me a greeting, it would have laid the gossip to rest." His tone was biting, warning her that she would have a difficult time placating him.

"You seemed to be exceedingly involved," Eleanor replied. "I took it as a sign that you wished to be ignored. You seem to have been kept so busy that *you,* my very dear husband, could find neither the time nor the energy to be here to greet your so-sadly-missed wife on her arrival today." Her yellow-green eyes blazed now, her resentment at the provocation he had offered her beginning to overcome her gentler feelings. "Our dear friend, Lady Codface, seems to have kept you so close to her side that you had not the least inclination to present yourself here, if only to assure yourself that we had arrived safely."

"You managed to console yourself with Jeremy's presence," he retorted. "He was most attentive to you. Don't let his attentions make you forget that you are married, dear wife." Geoffrey moved toward her and reached out to caress her cheek. "You looked very well tonight. I must compliment you on your appearance."

"Don't waste your breath, my lord. Your compliments seem to carry a sting with them and are usually a signal that you want something from me." Eleanor drew back from her husband. His closeness was having a dizzying effect on her. Her pulse had begun to quicken, and the tremble of desire had begun within her body. "Please, leave me alone. I want nothing to do with you tonight."

"Perhaps you would rather have had Jeremy visit you?"

"Jeremy? What do you..." Understanding came to Eleanor. "You are despicable! When did I ever give you the slightest inkling that I am the kind of woman who would have an affair with her husband's best and truest friend! I am no Alvinia Coddington, to lie with any man who professes to want me. Get out of here, get out!" Eleanor raised her hands, and beat the earl's chest in rage and despair.

"Take care, Eleanor, take care." Geoffrey grabbed Eleanor's wrists and pulled her hands to her sides. "Don't try to hurt me. You'll only hurt yourself." He held her immobile, gazing into her face, studying her lips, her eyes, the contours of her cheeks. He realized that she had right on her side when she berated him for his not being present to greet her earlier. Knowing he was wrong only irritated him and evoked a stronger desire to punish *her* for being right.

He could feel the rapid flutter of the pulse in her wrists even as his eyes noticed the movement at the base of her throat. His eyes flared with desire, changing from the color of a stormy sea to the limpid violet-gray of passion. Slowly he drew her closer, transferring both her wrists to one hand as he let his other hand move about her waist. She struggled against his hold, exciting him further until he lowered his head and took her lips with his.

Languor began to steal over Eleanor as her body responded to the sweet pressure of Geoffrey's mouth. Her rage gradually changed to need. Her lips opened and her tongue moved in answer to his. Slowly and surely his assault on her senses provoked a stronger and stronger response from her. He began to caress her body, his fingers roaming at will over the thin chiffon that separated her silky skin from his touch. The hand that had been holding hers let go to grasp her hip and pull her body closer to his. She felt the strength of his arousal. His fingertips kneaded the tender flesh, then drifted to her breast, playing a delicate tattoo against the turgid tip.

She gasped at the sensation and leaned against his hard body as her knees lost their strength. "No, no . . . you mustn't . . ." she moaned against his mouth before opening again to his questing kiss. Her body was in flames. At last her arms wound around his neck as she moved her hips in an undulating motion against his.

Suddenly they were frantic in their need for each other. Hands tore at clothing, pulled at buttons, yanked at ties until their two bodies strained against each other, naked flesh to naked flesh. Hurrying, straining, tugging, exciting, each urged the other with hands, mouth, tongue, and voice to attain that miraculous ecstasy.

"Geoffrey, oh, Geoffrey, touch me again like that," Eleanor pleaded.

"Yes . . . yes . . . yes. Linnet, my Linnet . . . now . . . now."

In a crescendo of unutterable beauty, they shared a moment that could never be memorized, but would always be remembered.

In the aftermath they lay drowsy and momentarily at peace. Eleanor continued to caress Geoffrey's chest through the mat of reddish fur, then touched his face, relishing his lean, angular chin and cheekbones. He stroked her back, turning on his side so that he could better hold her in his arms, occasionally setting a gentle kiss on her mouth or breast. Soon they fell into a deep sleep, waking some time later to find themselves chilled.

Geoffrey pulled the duvet over his wife. She reached up and touched his cheek in a loving gesture. He took hold of her fingers. "If you continue to flirt with other men, wife," he whispered, "I shall take it as a signal that you are in need of my attentions. Tonight will be repeated as often as you make a spectacle of yourself."

"What—what are you saying? Are you joking?"

"No. Merely telling you to conduct yourself with an eye to counting the cost of your lavishly endowed 'melting glances.'"

Eleanor went cold with fury. Her skin flushed, then turned white. Her breath seemed to leave her body. "You don't know what you've done, Geoffrey." Her voice was unexpectedly calm. "You'll never have me again. I loathe you. You've taken whatever love may have been growing between us and destroyed it more completely than if you had destroyed me. It's too bad that we still have to see one another on occasion. I shall do my best to avoid you." Feeling as though the body that had so recently been flushed with love were now encased in the same ice that seemed to fill her heart, Eleanor turned her back on him and closed her eyes.

Geoffrey was startled by Eleanor's denunciation. He looked over at her still body for a moment, then returned to his room.

His damned pride . . . why had he opened his mouth and said that? He knew she had no intention of doing more than being pleasant to Jeremy. And he knew as well that Jeremy was too good a friend to play him false with his wife. Then what imp of Satan had taken hold of his tongue and put those words into his mouth? How could he make it up to her?

He turned and peered into the shaving mirror atop his dressing table. "What are you fighting against, your lordship?" he addressed his image. "Are you so frightened by one slim, dark-haired beauty that you must serve her a mortal wound after having taken her without a by-your-leave? And what of her response? Wasn't it warm enough for you? Have you ever held a woman who was so pliable in your arms, so responsive to your needs, so . . . loving? And you, your lordship, what are your feelings towards the lady? Can it be you're afraid to acknowledge them? A coward, my lord. Not the cock of the walk, but a coward! Pfaugh! You disgust me, Geoffrey Amis William Edward de Maine. You disgust me!"

The earl sank into his soft feather mattress, hoping to fall asleep but suspecting that his thoughts would harass him for much of the night.

The next morning Eleanor, looking a trifle peaked, called for a hackney and prepared to leave the gray stone mansion. She had finally decided it was time to pay a call on her man of business. The benefits to Phillip of having the earl recognize him might be outweighed by the disadvantage to herself.

Last night had left her empty. More than ever before she was forced to acknowledge her deep love for her husband. But just when she had been ready to declare that love, he had dealt her a blow from which she thought she might never recover.

In the shocking accusation he had made after their passionate lovemaking, he had expressed virulent animosity. That any man could so accost a lover after such a moment must be a declaration of his true feelings. Thank God she hadn't told him of her love. Never would she, by word or look, so much as tender him a nod of accord, an instant of approbation. They were enemies. He had made it so. And if she found she was unable to create a life for herself while still living as his wife, she would take Phillip and leave him. To Hades with his earldom, his castle, his pride, his...everything! *She* would not be used this way. Let him continue to take his pleasure with Alvinia.

Parkins helped Eleanor into the deep blue redingote she had chosen to wear over a pale sprigged muslin round gown. Her ballibuntl straw bonnet had matching blue ribbons that tied under her chin. As the butler held open the door for her, he murmured an inquiry about when to expect her return, to which she replied that he could expect her when he saw her. The majordomo's face twitched imperceptibly at the answer.

Mr. Ferret's office was in the City, the oldest section of London where all the banking houses were located and all the institutions having to do with world trade. The driver steered carefully around several standing vehicles that were blocking the narrow street until he could find a space to draw into. Reaching into her reticule, Eleanor found the change to pay him and asked him to wait for her return.

Quickly she entered the venerable building that housed the offices of Ferret, Musgrove, Baldwig and Ferret and followed a graceful oak stairway up one flight of stairs. There the young countess was accosted by a clerk dressed in a sack coat with muslin cuffs tied around his arms to protect his sleeves from inkstains and dust.

"May I 'elp you, mum?" he asked.

"Would you be so kind as to direct me to Mr. Ferret, please? I am the Countess Hellistone."

"Hif you would be so good as to sit yerself down 'ere, my lady, I shall 'ave 'im 'ere tireckly," was the agreeable answer.

The clerk deftly pulled out a chair for Eleanor at a round mahogany table. He disappeared for several minutes, arriving back with a small tray containing a cup of tea and a small cake. Once he had served her, he gave her the message that Mr. Ferret would be available in a moment.

Eleanor waited patiently for the lawyer to make his appearance. In the quiet that pervaded the room, she was able to give her attention to the possible alternatives she had vis-à-vis her marriage and her relationship with Phillip. That Geoffrey would never hurt her again as he had last night was of primary importance. Whether she would continue to live with him in what would be a marriage of convenience was the decision to be made. As she considered the possibilities open to her, Eleanor found her memory of her husband intruding. She could see him at play with Phillip, running around the Long Gallery, letting the boy catch him, and then giving him a great hug. She could see him in the high-backed wing chair in front of the fireplace in the blue salon, reading to his mother and herself after dinner. She could see him, with tenderness on his face, reaching for her in the privacy of their bed, in that sweet moment after making love. What had happened to that man? Where had he gone, leaving the cruel stranger who had faced her last night?

"My dear Miss Glyndon . . . Oh, your pardon—I had forgot for the moment. Countess Hellistone, how are you?" A short, slender man of middle years had entered the chamber. He was dressed in an olive-green jacket and knee breeches of a fashion a touch out-of-date but correct. His sober appearance was enlivened by the pale gold-and-olive-striped waistcoat that peeked from beneath his jacket, and a pleasant twinkle relieved his plain features. "It's been quite a while since I've had the pleasure of attending you. I'm glad you took my advice and presented yourself to your husband. Is all going well?"

"Dear Mr. Ferret." Eleanor rose to take the hand offered to her. "I've been remiss in not having invited you to Hellistone House before this. Mrs. Ogden sends her best wishes. I believe she misses the fierce games of whist the two of you enjoyed." She let him lead her into another room, this one a spacious office furnished with a large oak desk, several chairs, a sofa, and a few tables. The walls were covered with books, paintings, sketches, and maps. A large window looked out over a mews at back of the building, and the sounds of the street were distant and unobtrusive.

"Ah yes, dear Mrs. Ogden. I'm glad she is well." Mr. Ferret saw that Eleanor was seated comfortably and then moved behind the desk to take his own chair. "Now, then, what may I do for you today? Something for the boy? Or do you want to transfer some funds to your husband's name?"

"No, Mr. Ferret. I came because . . . because . . . I don't

really know why. I think it was a mistake to present myself to Lord de Maine and prevent his marriage to Lady Coddington. He still seems to love her and . . . and I can't live with his having her as his *chère amie,* appearing with her at the same events to which I am invited, flaunting her as though he has no responsibility to me." Tears blurred Eleanor's hazel eyes. "It's ridiculous. When I first decided to inform the earl that he was married to me, I expected that we would be able to live together compatibly and might even come to have a regard for each other. I knew my arrival would be a blow to him, that he must have suffered some accident to have forgotten our wedding, and that he would have a difficult time in resolving the situation to his satisfaction. But the young man I remembered who was so kind, helpful, and gallant does not exist. He has become—or perhaps always was—unbearable. He turns hot and cold without warning. Before we came to London, I thought we were managing well and that he might even have . . . well, that was a dream.

"In any case," Eleanor continued, "after being most affectionate, he suddenly began to eschew my company and left abruptly for London. Until last evening I hadn't seen him in three weeks, and when I did see him, he was escorting Lady Coddington. Their actions were blatant and insulting to me and to my son!" Eleanor could no longer contain her rage. "I want to know how to divorce him! I refuse to go on with this farcical marriage, especially after last night."

"My dear Eleanor, my dear Eleanor." Mr. Ferret was clearly nonplused by her news. "I never dreamed that the situation was so grave. Are you certain that this is not a mere aberration, a temporary mood on your husband's part. We know, you and I, that some people don't share our standards. Perhaps it is merely his way of . . . of . . . expressing his—"

"His what, Mr. Ferret? There's no excuse for what

he did or what he said last night. He as much as told me that I was his bondswoman and had to do as he wished regardless of my own desires, and that he had the license to be with whomever he chose, wherever he chose, whenever he chose. I have no say in the matter." As she spoke, Eleanor hit the arm of her chair with her fist in time to her words. "I will not live like that! Miss Shappley didn't save my life and teach me all she did so that I could waste away in a miserable marriage. I won't do it, I won't. You must help me find a way out."

"I would if I could, you know that. But at the very least, it would take an act of Parliament to grant your divorce, and in this instance, your husband would have to divorce you. He is the one with influence. In the eyes of Society, you are no one. You have station only because of his name.

"Perhaps if I were to speak to him," Mr. Ferret suggested. "With the greatest diplomacy, to be sure. It might be possible to effect an amicable agreement so that you could be excused from being in the same place and at the same time as he."

"I suppose it would be a concession that might make my life more tolerable. But I don't think he would go along with any such idea. I've discovered he has a great deal of pride and that it gives him an overweening self-esteem." Eleanor's voice expressed a touch of malice. She was silent for a while, her head down, her body slumped in her chair. "I really wish things might have been better. He is so easy to love when he forgets to be the earl." The last was uttered in a whisper.

Mr. Ferret said nothing. He found Eleanor's last statement most interesting. Could it be that the countess—it was hard to think of the young girl he first knew as such a grand lady—was in love with her husband? Her anger was extreme, especially considering that at the very first, she had indicated she would look only for a marriage of convenience.

Miss Shappley had entrusted Eleanor to his care, and he had advised her to the best of his ability. He had brought to her attention the necessity of having Phillip recognized by his father, and he had encouraged her to show herself when she had preferred to remain unknown to the earl. He had realized that Eleanor had been half in love with Geoffrey then. Now there was a strong possibility that she had succumbed to him completely.

Now it was up to him to save the day. The lawyer exhorted himself go to it with speed.

"Eleanor," he began, "is it possible for you to continue as you are for a few weeks? Just to see whether this is a passing phase, a last gasp, as it were?"

"I suppose I could," she replied hesitantly. "But I won't promise to live with him as a true wife. I fully intend to lock my door to him and . . . and . . . Oh, Mr. Ferret, I shouldn't be speaking to you of such things."

"My dear girl, who else shall you speak to? I have always considered you the daughter I never had. Your late benefactress instructed me to watch over you, and I have done so to the best of my ability. You must know that all of us need confidants at one time or another. This is your time to have someone in whom you can confide. Now, go home, take up your life, and have as enjoyable a time as possible. You may as well take advantage of the gaiety of the season. If the situation doesn't take a turn for the better, we can talk further in two or three weeks."

Mr. Ferret arose from his chair and gave Eleanor his arm as he led her to the door. "Do please give my warmest regards to Mrs. Ogden. Do you think she would allow me to take tea with her one afternoon?"

"I'm sure she would love to see you." Before she left the room, Eleanor reached up and placed a grateful kiss on Mr. Ferret's cheek. "Thank you for your time and attention, sir. I feel better for having talked with you. I look forward to seeing you at Hellistone House, and I know Mrs. Ogden will also."

Eleanor returned to Hellistone House in a more optimistic frame of mind. Perhaps Mr. Ferret had been right. He, being a man, would better understand another man. It was possible that Geoffrey was merely squirming at the newly discovered bonds of matrimony. She would wait before doing anything drastic. If only she didn't love him so much. If only he returned her love. But never, during the tenderest moments they shared, had he ever intimated that he had the slightest affection for her. If truth be known, last night she had felt more like a light-skirt than a spouse when she had awakened to find him gone from her bed without having offered the loving words she needed.

Enough of this! No more repining! From now on she would become the brightest, most social, most courted wife in London. And if her husband wasn't doing the courting, well...no one need know that her heart was breaking.

CHAPTER EIGHT

ELEANOR PAUSED FOR a moment in front of the magnificent portrait by Gainsborough of Lady Anne Winterset.
"Amazing how he was able to convey the sweet look on
her face," she commented. "I don't think there are any
portraitists today who could do as well." She turned to
Jeremy Broadbent for his opinion.

"It's hard to tell. Our greatest artists today seem more
inclined to paint landscapes. Have you seen any of Mr.
Turner's works?" Jeremy strolled alongside her as he
spoke, surveying the rest of the exhibit that was on display at the Royal Academy of Art. "You know he has
his own gallery. But he's a strange man. I've heard he's
not the most cordial fellow."

"I haven't met him, but I admire his paintings exces-
sively, " Eleanor replied. "Shall we look at the Con-
stables once more before we leave? I think Mr. Turner
probably resents having to answer questions put to him
by people like ourselves when he would much rather be
at work putting color on canvas." Eleanor gave a little
shiver and draped her Norwich shawl more securely about
her shoulders. The weather had been quite chilly for late
May.

"My lady, have you taken a chill?" Jeremy inquired.
"It's quite cool in here. A vast room like this holds the
winter cold well on into summer. I really think we ought
to leave. We can return for another visit when the weather

warms up." He drew her towards the outer hall. "I didn't mention it to you earlier, but if you would like, Countess Lieven mentioned that she was 'at home' this afternoon and asked that we stop by. She knows Lady Imogene and wishes to meet you. Do you care to go?"

"Would it be proper to bring me as a guest, Jeremy?"

"In this instance, yes. The countess may usually be found surrounded by the most interesting people. Besides the members of the *beau monde,* she enjoys bringing together artists and writers. Sometimes she encourages an informal musicale. In fact, I heard one of the most marvelous baritone voices at her home. If you will believe me, it belonged to your husband. Very fine voice, that."

"Lady Imogene mentioned that he sang, but not how well. I haven't had the pleasure. Well, if you're sure the countess won't object to my appearance . . . I've met her only once and that was at Almack's the other evening. Shall we retrieve our cloaks?"

Jeremy had arranged for Eleanor to view the present exposition of paintings and sculpture at the Academy, knowing her love of the arts. He had become her favorite escort these past few weeks. Geoffrey was present at only the most important affairs. Occasionally Eleanor would meet her husband at a rout or gala at someone's home where he would greet her curtly, maintaining the cold politeness that had become habitual with him. Since that bitter night when he had told her of his disregard for her, she had avoided any further contact with him.

Of late, however, she had noticed a smoldering in his eyes whenever he saw her with Jeremy. He had made no comment on his good friend's attendance on Eleanor, but there seemed to be a warning implicit in his angry glances.

As thoughts about her husband went through her head, Eleanor accepted the large sable muff from her escort and finished buttoning her pelisse. The warm wine color of the coat and its matching bonnet cast a rosy glow over her features. She smiled as she shared a glance of anticipation with her companion. "I'm really looking forward to seeing the Lieven's home," she said. She made a moue and wrinkled her nose. "I feel like a country chick come to the city for the first time to enjoy the sights! Hopeless really. No matter how many people I meet and no matter how many great homes I am invited to, I always want to ooh and ahh at the sights. Do you think I shall ever change?"

"I should hope not!" was Jeremy's immediate answer. "Part of your charm is that you don't know everything about everything. There are still things your gentlemen admirers can teach you!" Jeremy handed a coin to the doorman as they walked out of the building. "There's my carriage. Duncan was able to maintain his place at the curb." He raised his cane to call his groom's attention.

"Do you really think I have admirers, Jeremy?" Eleanor gave him a flirting glance as he helped her into the coach.

"Certainly. There isn't a man that meets you who wouldn't like to slay Geoffrey for having found you first. You may consider me one of your most faithful *cicisbeos*, always ready to place my heart and my fortune at your feet." With an exaggerated gesture he placed his hand over the general area of his heart, illustrating his readiness to pluck it from its place.

The elegant Countess de Maine gave a little chuckle. "Really, Jeremy, your nonsense always makes me laugh. It is so good to have you as a friend. I don't seem able to confide in many people. Everyone I've met seems to be so concerned with the frivolities of life. It becomes so boring to sustain conversations with them. How did you and I escape that situation?"

"Because we are originals. You have no sensibilities, and I have discrimination." Jeremy's usually angelic expression took on a mock satanic cast. "I know enough not to take up with the loose fish of our caste, and you are too intelligent to want to."

"I shall take what you are saying as funning," Eleanor replied lightly. "If you were serious, I might have to castigate your bad manners! Now, no more of such talk. I wish you to tell me about the Count and Countess Lieven. Were they not instrumental in convincing Prinny to send Sir Gregory to St. Petersburg?" Eleanor settled back on the seat and prepared to discuss politics and diplomacy with Jeremy.

Before they had thoroughly explored the subject, the carriage drew up at the St. James's Square home of the ambassador from Russia and his wife. Moments later, Eleanor and Jeremy divested themselves of their coats and were announced by the stately butler, who had escorted them to the crowded drawing room. Eleanor was stunned to see the size of the crowd standing around in groups of two or three engaged in vociferous conversation. From time to time a voice somewhat louder than the rest would call attention to a certain point of discussion. The groups would rearrange themselves, as if to a signal, and the conversations would be resumed.

Eleanor was astonished. "How does anyone hear what anyone else is saying?" she asked. "It sounds like the Tower of Babel!"

"It's rare that they want to hear anyone other than themselves," Jeremy replied. "I've been told that this is the best place to come if you want to say the most outrageous things without having to pay the penalty for having said them!" Jeremy laughed at the horrified look on Eleanor's face.

"But I thought we were coming to hear and participate in an orderly discussion. This is amazing." She watched wonderingly for a while, attempting to find her host and hostess in the throng. She caught bits and pieces of conversations about new novels just off the presses—

Frankenstein by Mary Wollstonecraft Shelley and *The Bride of Lammermoor* by Sir Walter Scott. In more subtle tones, Byron's Fourth Canto of *Childe Harolde* was spoken of—less for its content and style than for the unconventional life of its author.

"There's the countess over by the archway, speaking with Lord Alvanley and 'Poodles' Byng," Jeremy pointed out. "Have you met them, Eleanor? Quite amusing fellows actually. 'Poodles' seems to be somewhat unusual, what with all his dogs, but he's really quite harmless and most obliging when he takes a liking to one."

Jeremy began moving through the crowd, drawing Eleanor after him. They had just reached the small group of people that had been his objective when a familiar voice was heard addressing them.

"Eleanor, dear wife, and Jeremy—have you just arrived? What a happy surprise." Dressed with a meticulousness that bordered on perfection, Geoffrey greeted his wife and his best friend. "Have you met the countess yet? I think, Jeremy, that I can take over the task of making the introductions. I do take pride in presenting Eleanor to the people I know." Geoffrey took her hand in his and raised it to his lips. With a mocking look in his eyes, he added, "You are so very special, dearest, and everyone is looking to meet the beautiful Countess de Maine." He put his arm around Eleanor's waist and guided her over to their hostess. "Countess Lieven, may I make you acquainted with my wife, Eleanor, Countess de Maine."

The short, dark-haired woman nodded her head graciously and, in a delightful accent, murmured her pleasure at meeting the wife of so romantic a fellow as her dear Geoffrey. "You were at Almack's last week, no? I admired your gown very much. So wonderful to be tall and able to wear such dresses, yes?" Having made this profound statement, the countess excused herself and moved slowly away.

Eleanor's eyes met Geoffrey's, and she began to giggle. She couldn't help herself. She tried to stifle the sound behind her handkerchief. "Is that the woman that has set the whole of European society agog?" She asked, helplessly overcome with mirth.

"Yes, I'm afraid so," Geoffrey replied with a twitch of his lips. "She's terribly *haut monde,* you know." He turned to one of the gentlemen standing near them and asked, "Poodles, how long did she bless you with her conversation? If I were unfamiliar with her manner, I might take offense. She's amazing. It's enough that she allows you to meet her. I think she believes Russia is the center of the world from whence cometh all things and people superior, and all other places are merely satellites to it."

A ripple of laughter rose from his listeners as he went on to introduce his wife to Mr. Byng and Lord Alvanley. As soon as polite acknowledgements had been made, Geoffrey drew Eleanor apart from the others.

"I did not expect to meet you here," he said. "Jeremy has quite taken you under his wing, has he not?" His lean, handsome face was turned away from her, but Eleanor sensed the intensity of his attention. "You will take care, won't you, my dear? I hold the name de Maine very precious and would want no stain upon the escutcheon because of your activities."

Her gasp was clearly audible even in the noisy room. The careless cruelty of his remark brought fresh pain in her heart. That he could even suspect her of so reprehensible an action, when she had never behaved with anything less than the greatest decorum.

"Sir, you are contemptible!" she sputtered. "I have *never* given you any reason to treat me so. If anyone were to complain, it should be I—*I* who have a husband who whores around as though he were yet unwed. Is this the behavior you will teach our son, my lord? Is he to follow in your footsteps?" Eleanor's voice was a hiss of sound reaching no farther than Geoffrey's ears. She watched his features darken slowly as his anger deepened. "You flaunt your *inamorata* without a thought for your mother or myself. Do you even care about the slights and gossip that we have been subject to? Don't blacken me with the same brush, *husband*. I care more about my name than you do. My name and my self-respect." She whirled away from him, slipping quickly through the crowd, her vision blurred by tears of ... anger ... regret ... and sorrow, because he was working so hard to kill what feeling she had for him.

She made her way to a small alcove on the other side of the room and remained there for several minutes as she tried to bring her tears under control. At last she felt more composed and moved to leave the small room. Before she parted the curtains that concealed the doorway, her husband appeared, a gleam of anger still on his face.

"I hope you are more in control of yourself now, madam," he said calmly. He walked to her side, ignoring her small movement away from him when he put a hand under her elbow and led her back to a seat near the window. "There are a few things that must be said. First of all, I would like to thank you for bringing the gossip and slights to you and my mother to my attention. I had not realized the situation was so extreme. Second, I wish to explain what action we will take in response. And I expect you to obey me implicitly. Do you understand?"

"Understand? Obey you? What do you mean?"

"Do you intend to go to Lady Selkirk's ball tonight?"

"Of course. Your mother accepted for both of us." Eleanor couldn't meet Geoffrey's eyes. She was too afraid that her own would give her away. "But what has that to do with anything?"

"There's only one way to put a halt to all this talk you seem to think is being bruited about. Tonight, when I bring Alvinia to your attention, you will be everything that is polite. Converse with her for a time and even walk around the room with her once or twice. Then, when—"

"Are you mad?" Eleanor demanded, rising hastily in her agitation. "How can you ask me to acknowledge your mistress? Have you no consideration, no thought for anyone but yourself?" She paced restlessly, unable to stay still. "I'll do no such thing. If you want someone to wave a wand over your . . . your . . . fish, then find another fairy godmother. It won't be me!"

The more Eleanor paced and the more distressed she became, the calmer Geoffrey seemed. He lounged back on the high-backed demi-sofa, crossed one leg over the other, and carefully straightened his sharply creased trouser leg. He examined his nails, rubbed them on the lapel of his jacket, then held them up to the light once more. "If you have any further objections," he drawled, "you might as well voice them now. I have time to sit and listen. Then we can get back to the course of action I intend for you to take." He watched as Eleanor tried to control herself, knowing that she was on the verge of doing something violent.

"I don't believe you," she cried. "How can you speak so—so . . . coolly when you know you are behaving like a—a—Oh, I can't even think of a word to describe you!"

"Is there anything else you would like to say?"

Eleanor gripped her hands tightly together and turned her back on him. As angry as she was, as much as she wanted to scream and carry on, there was still a corner of her mind that could appreciate the humor in the situation. A biting humor to be sure, but enough to cause the elusive dimple in her cheek to make a quick appearance.

Geoffrey seemed to sense her lightening mood, and his eyes softened when she turned back to him. He held out his hand. "Come, sit down and let us start afresh."

Eleanor hesitated before taking the offered hand. What was it about this man that went straight to her heart? She loved the look of him—his tall body, his coppery hair, his deeply creased cheeks, and his gray eyes that glinted with silver. But those were mere physical attributes. What was it about him that made him so special in her eyes? For most of the time since she had come back into his life, she had had to fight for his attention. When he seemed to forget whatever anger he held against her, he was wonderfully warm and friendly. The days when he had played with Phillip and her at Pentalwyn had been lovely days that gave her a glimpse of the man she had hoped him to be. But just when she thought things between them had finally begun to settle, he would change and that cold, closed look would appear on his face.

There was no doubt but that he could charm the leaves off a tree. Here he was charming her into doing exactly what she didn't want to do. How could he expect her to show the least degree of amity toward that...creature Alvinia? But if there could be peace between her husband and herself, she would do even that.

As Eleanor gazed intently at his face, Geoffrey returned the look. He saw before him a woman who was the epitome of his dreams—the slender, rounded body, the creamy skin, the large amber eyes and proudly held head, the softly curved lips that had returned his kisses with such passion. Why was he constantly at war with her? Why did he fight his attraction for her? She had much more to offer than any other woman he had ever known, and in bed she was a constant surprise, responding to his every need with a passion that matched and surpassed his. He felt the web she had woven about him. Was he afraid of being ensnared?

"Why do you look at me so?" Eleanor's voice broke into his thoughts.

"How do I look at you?"

"You—you examine me as though I were a species with which you were unfamiliar. I wish you would not. It is very . . . disconcerting."

"Then come and sit. I was not aware that I made you uncomfortable." He drew her down once more. "I would like you to go along with my request, Eleanor. Once the gossip is laid to rest, life will be easier all 'round. I don't ask you for Alvinia's sake or my own, but for my mother and yourself." As he spoke, his thumb caressed the palm of her hand, sending a wave of desire through her. "You must see it would be the right thing to do."

"Y-y-yes . . . I see." Suddenly she was breathless. Her body swayed toward Geoffrey's. Her eyes became soft, the lids heavy. Her mouth opened slightly, ready to receive his kiss.

She was like a magnet drawing him to her. His hand pulled at hers, bringing her closer to him, bringing her lips within reach. Their bodies remained apart, yet their lips met and tongues and breath as a heat enveloped them both. Flames leaped within them, almost blotting out an awareness of where they were until Geoffrey finally pulled away, regretfully, slowly. He took a deep breath and touched Eleanor's mouth, tracing her lips with a gentle finger.

"I wish we were at home. Then I need not stop," he murmured.

"Ummm," she answered. She let herself relish the evanescent moment for a few more seconds, then gradually forced herself to attend the reality of Geoffrey's request. She gave herself a tiny shake to dispel the magic, then said crisply, "Very well. For your mother's sake, I'll pretend a . . . a . . . friendship with Alvinia. But don't expect me to carry on the pretense for more than the one evening." She forced herself to stand and move away from Geoffrey. "I'm sure Jeremy is looking for me. It's past time for us to leave. Shall we see you at dinner tonight?"

"No, I fear I shall have to deny myself the pleasure. But later at Lady Selkirk's... save the first waltz for me." He rose and escorted her to the doorway. "Until this evening, then." Once more his lips touched hers with a quick, firm pressure, and then his hand against her back urged her from the alcove.

She walked slowly about the larger chamber, seeking her escort. Here and there she was urged to join a conversation, but she lingered only a moment before excusing herself. Just as she was beginning to wonder where Jeremy had gotten to, his voice sounded in her ear.

"I thought I had lost you in the crush," he said. "Are you ready to leave?"

"Oh yes, Jeremy. I had completely forgotten, Belle-mère and I are expected at Lady Selkirk's ball this evening, and I must get home to dress." Seeing a question in his eyes she gave him a bright smile, but chose not to answer it. "You must know by now that a woman needs at least two hours to prepare for a morning drive and twice that time for anything more grand!"

"To be sure, but the results are so pleasurable! It's worth every minute a gentleman might have to wait." Jeremy handed Eleanor her muff and conducted her from the crowded room. "I suspected you might be ready to leave, so I called for my carriage. It should be here by now."

"You are everything that one could want in a friend, Jeremy. Thank you."

"I only wish I had met you before my ever-fortunate friend." At Eleanor's startled gasp, he continued, "No, I won't importune you. I have too much respect for you to do that, my dear. But please know that, if ever you need anything that I can give you or do for you, you have only to ask."

"I know, Jeremy, and I thank you. I also know that you are as much Geoffrey's friend as mine, and that both of us can count on that friendship." Eleanor climbed gracefully into the waiting carriage, waited until Jeremy had settled himself beside her, and then changed the subject. "Are you going to Lady Selkirk's?" she asked.

"Now that I know you'll be there, of course. Will you save a dance for me?"

"Certainly, and you may take me in to supper." Once more on a less serious footing, Eleanor could relax her vigilance. Her life was given to Geoffrey, but she had no wish to hurt Jeremy. He was a good and dear friend, the brother she had never had, and she hoped she had been able to intimate as much to him. She let her head rest against the pale blue squabs, thinking about the request her husband had made. Dealing with Alvinia in a friendly way would be exceedingly difficult, but Eleanor supposed that even such difficulties could be overcome for one evening. She would take life a moment at a time and savor whatever happiness she found.

CHAPTER NINE

"MR. BRUMMEL, YOUR wit is too cruel to say that the lady had the air of a dying moth. Not even to give her the beauty of a butterfly! Too cruel by far." Lady Selkirk tapped Beau Brummel's wrist with her fan. "I shan't listen to another word about her. Oh, there, I do believe Lady Hellistone has arrived . . . and with her daughter-in-law."

She had by this time taken Mr. Brummel's arm and was moving toward the two ladies she had just sighted. "Come along, George, Jeremy Broadbent told me you were promised a dance with Lady de Maine. She is sure to attract a great deal of attention this evening, so you might as well put your name on her card before it's filled."

The large elaborate ballroom which Eleanor, accompanied by Lady Imogene and Mrs. Ogden, had just entered, was decorated like the inside of the tent of some sheik of Araby. Gaily striped cloth was swagged around the upper part of the walls and drawn into a billowing knot above the central chandelier. Thick rugs and tapestries hung on the walls supporting large brass-and-pewter reliefs that reflected the scintillating candles used to light the room. Several hundred people, the women in gowns in all the colors of the rainbow, were moving around the floor in a gay gavotte, accompanied by the sounds of a fourteen-piece musical ensemble located on a balcony above the crowd.

Lady Imogene pressed Eleanor's arm and whispered a warning about the approaching Mr. Brummel. "He's begun to lose some of his influence with Prinny, but he is still able to make or break a reputation among the *ton*. And, I must say, he can be a most engaging devil. Just be yourself. Don't try to impress him." She moved away from her daughter-in-law and greeted Lady Selkirk.

"Dear Sally, you're looking very well this evening. May I make you acquainted with my dear Eleanor. And Mr. Brummel, my son's wife, Lady de Maine." She watched the ensuing acknowledgments with a smile. In spite of her words to Eleanor, Lady Imogene had no worry that the younger woman would fail to make a place for herself among the *ton*.

Eleanor had chosen a gown of rich cream with a wide, draped décolletage. The bodice was caught beneath her breasts with a girdle of pearls woven with silver thread and delicate pink velvet ribbon. Pearls were also sewn in scattered handfuls across the layered silk gauze overskirt. Magnificent earrings of pearls and pink sapphires swung at either side of her face, accenting the classic line of her jaw. The pearl-and-sapphire circlet that held her chignon in place gave a regal quality to her person as she graciously accepted Mr. Brummel's compliments and Lady Selkirk's comments.

"Dare I hope you have a dance left for me, Lady de Maine?" asked Beau Brummel. "A mutual friend assured me that I would find no greater pleasure than to spend an hour in your company. Should I have the temerity to do that while in this sacred precinct, I fear the gossip would fly and your husband would call me out in the morning . . . and that could be the death of me!" Brummel wagged his finger at his listeners. "You shall not see such a drastic sight so quickly, although, of all the ladies I have met so far, Lady de Maine might most easily give me the incentive to do so foolish a thing. That is, of course, except for you, Lady Imogene, and you, Sally, and the delightful Lady Jersey and Lady Livermore and Lady ... ah, but I forget myself. You see, Lady de Maine, I am really a most accomplished flirt and fall immediately in love with all my companions and so must deny all so that none shall be unhappy."

A delicious trill of laughter issued from Eleanor's lips. Demurely, she replied that she was happy to be among so distinguished a company as the ladies mentioned by Mr. Brummel.

"Already I can tell that you are a lady of uncommon acumen, Lady de Maine," he replied. "Is your card already filled? If not, may I request the second and fifth dance, although I must confess to not dancing. I prefer to keep alive that almost-dead art of conversation. May I look forward to conversing with you?" Mr. Brummel lifted an eyebrow in question, his eyes gleaming with amusement.

"My dear sir, you flatter me more than I can tell you to single me out for such exceptional attention. Two dances ... What will the gossips say?" Eleanor's eyes twinkled. "However, I confess that I would like that above all else. Mr. Jeremy Broadbent has told me that, if you take me up, I shall be an unparalleled success!"

"Ah-h-h, wicked, Lady de Maine, wicked. To allow that you would accept my kind invitation for such a base reason. I am stricken to the heart." Mr. Brummel bowed low over Eleanor's hand. "Even so, O beauteous charmer, I shall allow you to use me. But only in my office of *arbiter elegantiarum,* you understand. Until later." Again Mr. Brummel bowed, then turned and sauntered away.

"Dearest Eleanor, you are made!" Mrs. Ogden chortled. "He is a most unexpected man. You would never believe the stories I have heard about him."

"Yes, once news of the Beau's attention makes the rounds, you may be certain that you will be considered the newest Incomparable," Lady Imogene agreed. "His cachet is even greater than my son's, and the best part is that he has never once recognized Alvinia's existence. In fact, he termed her a vulgarity not too long ago. Now, we must see that the rest of your card is filled." She turned about slowly, picking out those gentlemen she considered suitable for her daughter-in-law to meet. A glimmer of a smile and a slight nod of her head brought first one then another to be introduced to Eleanor.

Before long, every dance had been assigned, and two gentlemen were negotiating for the privilege of enjoying Eleanor's company during the interval. As the two men laughingly argued prior right to Eleanor's presence, a familiar velvety voice claimed the prerogative. "You actually promised me the first waltz and, as your husband, I claim the interval, my dear. You must remember..."

Eleanor stiffened as the Earl of Hellistone claimed her hand to lift it to his lips in greeting. "My lord," she managed to say, "it was my recollection that you were promised only if you arrived in time to sign my card before another asked and was accepted. 'Tis the early bird, after all..."

"Do you compare yourself to the lowly worm, my love? I will surely not allow that!" An unexpected twinkle in his gray eyes elicited a sound almost like a giggle from Eleanor's patrician throat. "Ah, you smile," he said. "I feel much more optimistic now. It is truly difficult for a lowly husband to become a contender for his wife's favors." The earl nodded to his two rivals, dismissing their title to his wife's company. "We have a few moments before the first dance commences. Shall we stroll for a while?" Without waiting for an answer, he tucked Eleanor's hand in the crook of his elbow and led her away.

"Are we to meet Alvinia now?" Eleanor asked, her laughter dropping away from her. "There's probably just enough time for me to say hello to her before the music begins."

"No hurry, Linnet. You'll find she's changed."

"Oh?"

"She doesn't like this talk any more than I do. It hasn't been easy for her, you know. First becoming a widow and finding that her husband had nothing to leave her, and then discovering that I was already married and unavailable to her just when she thought herself about to be wed. It was a terrible comedown for a very proud woman. Surely you must understand her feelings."

"Mmm."

"Is that all you can say?"

"What is it you wish me to say?"

Eleanor's question silenced Geoffrey. What *did* he wish her to say? Damn, why had he been so pigheaded in the first place? What was he trying to do? He wasn't really interested in Alvinia. If truth be known, she had become rather a shrew and was no longer the cool, sophisticated woman he had once planned on marrying. She had urged him to insist that Eleanor make peace with her, saying that the scandal would be laid to rest that way. But he really didn't care. Seeing Eleanor earlier today, the center of an admiring group, and again tonight, with the men vying for her attention, had brought home his own need for her. He had been fighting it all along, afraid to admit that he had fallen victim to a woman's charms.

"I wish for you to be polite, that's all. Simply acknowledge her and exchange a few words with her. I insist upon that, Eleanor." He watched her face lose its pleasant expression. "No, I didn't mean that. I don't insist. I ask you most respectfully."

Now Eleanor gazed at him with astonishment. What was he up to? *Asking* her most respectfully! Was he planning a divorce? Was this all some ploy to make her the butt of his animosity? Anger flared, then was tempered with sadness. Perhaps it was for the better. She couldn't stand this kind of warfare much longer. Mrs. Ogden had suggested she try to make him jealous. Well, perhaps she would do just that. It had best be a stranger, one who had no friendship with Geoffrey. At least she might force him into declaring himself one way or the other, and this terrible uncertainty would end.

"Very well," Eleanor agreed. "I shall be all that is polite."

"You shan't be sorry, Eleanor. I promise."

Well, at least he no longer sounded like an enemy, she decided. What heaven if he changed from the erratic, irrational man she had known these past few months and became the gentle, loving husband she longed for. They could be so happy. He loved Phillip, she knew. If only he could love her. Well, she would give it her last chance. Give it all or nothing, make or break. If he had any feelings for her at all, he'd fight to hold on to her.

The tall, handsome man and his lovely wife continued to stroll around the room. From a distance away, Lady Imogene's curious eyes watched the two stop to speak to a vivacious blonde and a rather interesting-looking dark-haired man. She wondered what maggot had gotten into her son's head that he was encouraging his wife and his inamorata to meet and chat. And who was Alvinia's escort? He had an air of... mischief about him. He was a foreigner, no doubt.

The conversation that Lady Imogene wondered about was very polite and very conventional until Alvinia introduced the Comte de Rochfort. Dark, satanic eyebrows rose above equally dark eyes as the Frenchman raised his quizzing glass to study Countess de Maine.

"Madame." He bent his head and brought her hand to his lips. *"Je suis enchanté de faire votre connaisance. Your wife, m'sieu, is of the first stare, n'est-ce pas?"*

"You are too kind, *m'sieu le comte,* too kind," Geoffrey answered. "How are you this evening, Alvinia?"

"La, Geoffrey, you of all people should know that."

Good God, the woman actually simpered! Eleanor thought.

Without actually pushing Eleanor aside, Alvinia managed to edge up to Geoffrey in such a way that his wife found herself standing beside the French count. "Have you been in England long?" she asked, trying to converse politely.

"Oui, madame, since three years. I have the plans to return to France as soon as your gracious *gouvernement* rewards me with the titles to my estates." His black eyes glittered under the many-candled chandelier. "Do you stay long in London?"

"I . . . don't know. My husband hasn't decided."

"I would wish that I had met you earlier this evening, when still you had a waltz left open. It is too late to hope for one?"

Eleanor gave a quick sidelong glance at Geoffrey, who was deep in conversation with Alvinia. If that was the amount of attention she could expect from him, he could whistle for his wife when next he wanted her!

"I have written my husband's name in for the next one, m'sieu," Eleanor answered, "but he is so busy, I'm sure he won't mind if I change it for yours." She glanced at the Frenchman's cynical mouth and thought to herself that she might be getting into something chancier than she expected.

"If I were your husband, madame," he said, "I would challenge anyone so ready to tempt providence." His dark eyes ranged over her figure admiringly. "You are a treasure to be cared for, my lady."

A shudder of . . . fear . . . loathing . . . what? swept through Eleanor. Suddenly she wished she had refused his request for a dance. The thought of his arm about her waist in the intimacy of the waltz was distasteful to her. Her only defense against such feelings was to treat his compliments lightly. Laughing, she tapped his wrist with her fan and told him that such statements were too fulsome and not for so simple a nature as hers.

"You are like the English rose, exquisitely pure and beautiful beyond compare."

"Please, you embarrass me," she protested. "I prefer you not tell me such things." Eleanor looked about at her husband, hoping he would see her distress and come to her rescue, but he seemed much too interested in Lady Coddington.

"Come, my lady, the music starts and you have given me this dance. Shall we?" The Frenchman held out his hand and waited for her to extend hers. Hesitantly, wishing herself elsewhere, Eleanor placed her cold fingers in his.

In an attempt to lighten her mood, Eleanor began to chatter. "I can't wait to try the floor," she said. "This is my first time on it, you know. Don't you think the musicians are splendid?" She stiffly followed de Rochfort's lead, whirling in the swooping figures of the dance. "Where do you stay in London, sir?"

"You are adorable, madame. So shy, like a young deer, ready to fly at the first sign of danger. You must not be afraid of me. I wish only to worship at your feet." He smiled at her, intimating that his wishes involved more activity than quiet worship. "Now, let me show you how the waltz is danced in Paris." With no further conversation, he whirled her away to the beat of the music. His hand, placed firmly but properly two inches above her waist, signaled each move he wished her to make. Not once did he attempt to hold her more closely than convention allowed, nor did he engage in any more speech that was overly intimate. Despite the circumspect character he now seemed to present, his hand burned through Eleanor's gown, and his eyes kept measuring her reactions. She felt almost like a pullet being prepared for a feast, a most unfamiliar and unpleasant feeling!

At last the dance was over, and Eleanor was able to move away from the comte. Forcing herself to walk slowly, she smiled agreeably and said she had enjoyed herself.

"But of course, how could you not?" The man's assurance and vanity astounded her. "I hope we shall meet again before the evening is over. Will you drive with me tomorrow?"

"Oh, I don't think I can. Geoffrey said something about..." As she was forming her excuse, Eleanor looked around the floor, hoping once again to signal her husband to rescue her. Instead, she saw him leaning over Alvinia, sharing what seemed to be an intimate conversation. The woman's hand was on his arm, and they stood closer together than they would have been had they been dancing. That did it! What was sauce for the goose...

"Oh, he was speaking of the next day, not tomorrow," she amended with false brightness. "Of course I would love to go driving with you. At what time?"

"Shall we make it for the morning promenade? About eleven?"

"Perfect. I shall be waiting for you. And now here comes Mr. Broadbent. He is my partner for the next dance."

Eleanor greeted Jeremy gratefully and hurried to join a set for the quadrille before the Frenchman could make any further remarks.

Now that Eleanor had accepted his invitation to go driving, she was already trying to decide whether she could plead a forgotten previous appointment or if she should come down with a desperate illness. No, those were definitely not the answers. Her presence was expected at Lord and Lady Minthrop's rout tomorrow night. If only she could return to Cornwall where she wouldn't get caught in all these machinations. And all because Geoffrey was such a... such a—

"Eleanor, where are you?" Jeremy's voice penetrated

her inattention. "It's very difficult to accomplish the complexities of this set without one's partner attending the proceedings—in mind as well as in person."

"Oh, Jeremy, I'm so sorry." They were separated for the moment by the configuration of the dance. When they came together again, Eleanor smiled at her partner and asked his pardon. "I've done something that might prove to be rather foolish, and it took my attention away from all of this." She gestured toward their surroundings.

"Is it something that I can help you with?"

"I wish you could, but I'm afraid not," she said regretfully. "I've accepted the comte's invitation to go driving tomorrow, and I find I would prefer not to."

"Has he done anything to displease you?" Jeremy suddenly sounded very protective. "You can tell him you've simply changed your mind."

"I don't think that would be at all polite. I will in all likelihood enjoy myself..." She tried to sound hopeful. "Please, forget that I said anything at all about it."

"As you wish. But I think the bounder has some nerve, inviting you out when he's just made your acquaintance. It's not done with a lady such as yourself."

Eleanor changed the subject lightly, knowing that Jeremy's protective instincts would keep him rumbling and grumbling about the comte for the rest of their dance together. At last she led his attention away from the Frenchman by accusing him of courting the newest debutante on the scene.

"'Pon honor, no such thing," he denied. "She's a taking chit, but at least twelve years my junior and terribly naïve. She makes me feel like her father. But she's quite pretty, quite."

"Oh dear, I think my knight is being drawn to another. You had best be careful, Jeremy." Eleanor breathed a sigh of relief as she greeted her next partner.

Not until after the interval did Eleanor once more speak with her husband. She had been about to waltz with a young man who had pleaded that she accept his partnering when a rich voice said, "I've come to claim a husband's privilege, Mr. Humboldt. You will have to find yourself another partner for this dance."

Eleanor turned to face Geoffrey and was about to speak when the music started. His eyes seemed to caress her. She could almost feel the pressure of his glance as it roved over her face and shoulders, pausing for an instant on her lips and then the pulse at the base of her neck. She read desire in the earl's eyes. Had she seen a sign of tenderness, or even a warmth that hinted at more than a lustful wanting, she might not have wanted to run from him.

"Now, Geoffrey," she began, "you know it's not very nice to steal me from Mr. Humboldt like that. We can dance another time. Come, Mr. Humboldt, the music has commenced. Shall we dance?" Quickly, Eleanor drew the startled young man away from the earl, hoping that her husband would accept her denial.

"Geoffrey, it doesn't look as though you've had too much success with your wife."

The earl lifted his quizzing glass slowly as he turned and peered through it at Beau Brummel's smiling face.

"Don't try to crush me with that glass, m'boy. Better try to teach birds to suck eggs! You forget, I taught you how to use that demmed thing, and ain't no one can use it with as much style as I!" Brummel brushed an invisible particle of dust from his jacket. "I like the lady. She has a delightful manner about her. Take care that she don't play too deep a game with that Rochfort fella. He's not got a good reputation. I should not wish to see either of you hurt, but she's a gel of spirit and might decide that, as long as *you* play at marriage, *she* might take the same road. Oh well, I should know better than to warn you. *Chacun à son goût,* as our French friends say." The great man moved casually away from the earl, waving a languid hand in farewell.

The earl leaned against one of the supporting columns and watched the dancers. It took him a moment to find his quarry's dark head, but, once found, it became the only head he saw. He watched as the cream-colored form moved gracefully through the crowd, dipping and twirling as her partner guided her. Her eyes shone as she smiled at the young man, tugging Geoffrey's heart and bringing a black look to his eyes.

When the dance finally ended in a burst of genteel laughter and a patter of applause, he pulled himself erect and once more moved around the room. Wryly he wondered at himself. He would have to woo his wife, court her with all the games that men and women play before acceding to the demands of marriage. Unfortunately, he had the next dance with Alvinia, which might undermine whatever slight progress he hoped to make with Eleanor.

Without making it apparent, Eleanor's gaze had followed Geoffrey during the last dance. She wondered at his pursuit of her. Something seemed to have changed in his manner, but not enough. When Mr. Humboldt had whirled her around in the waltz, stepping frequently on her feet, she found herself wishing fervently that she had accepted her spouse's request that she dance with him. He, at least, seemed to know where not to trod, as she remembered from another time. Her more kindly thoughts about the errant earl came to an abrupt halt when she saw him lead Alvinia out onto the floor. A flush of anger enflamed her.

My God, she was so jealous. It was impossible to feel such anger over a man on whom her only hold was the child she had borne him. If only it were herself he was holding, she should probably faint with an excess of emotion. Eleanor wrinkled her nose at the earl as she tried to let her sense of humor pacify her seemingly irrational emotions.

"Dear Mr. Venner," she said to her next partner before the music began, "would you be so good as to see me

back to Lady Imogene? I have the most terrible migraine,
that I must ask you to excuse me from the lancers. I fear
I shall have to go home."

"Certainly, Lady de Maine. I hope it is nothing. May
I call for your carriage for you?" The young man looked
stricken that she should have been overcome by that
elusive malady called "migraine" while in his company.

"If you would be so good. And do not feel that anything you have done has caused it. I have been feeling
unwell all evening." Eleanor tried to assure her partner
as they walked toward Lady Imogene. "Perhaps you would
call the day after tomorrow, and we can go riding together."

"That would of all things be the best, Lady de Maine."
The young man turned bright red with delight. "I shall
be the envy of all my friends. They bet me that I couldn't
even get you to dance with me, but this will be even
better."

"You bet, Mr. Venner? On a lady's name?" Eleanor
clicked her tongue at the embarrassed youth. "But then,
I suppose all men do such things. But if I were you, I
should never, never let the lady in question find out about
it. It could be considered an insult, you know."

"Oh . . . but I . . . never insult . . . ex—excuse me . . .
Here's Lady Imogene. I'll call for your carriage." He
ran as though being chased.

"My dear, what was that all about?" Lady Imogene
was sitting with her friend Lady Darcy. "Why aren't you
dancing?"

"Would you mind very much if we were to leave,
Belle-mère? I have the most awful headache." Eleanor
touched her forehead with a long, white hand. "Mr. Venner has been so kind as to call for the coach. If you would
like to stay . . ."

"No, no . . . not at all. Lady Darcy and I have just
about picked apart everyone who is anyone, and there's
nothing else to discover tonight." She turned to her friend

with a laugh. "You will excuse us, Phenella. I'll make arrangements tomorrow for the theater. I want to see the new production at Covent Garden."

The ladies made their farewells and quickly found their way out of the ballroom. A solicitous Mr. Venner helped them into their coach, offering to accompany them but relieved at their refusal. With many apologies if he had done anything to have disrupted the evening for Lady de Maine, and much stammering and stuttering, he finally bowed himself away.

"Well, what was that all about?" Lady Imogene asked. "A younger young man I'm sure I've never seen. Or is it just that I am getting older?" She leaned back with a sigh. "Why are we leaving so early, m'dear?"

"I couldn't stand there any longer, Belle-mère. The bright lights and the noise... suddenly they became too much and my head started to pound. I hope you didn't want to stay longer."

"Not at all. I'm just as relieved to go home as you are. Did you enjoy your dance with de Rochfort? He's quite the gallant, isn't he?"

"Very handsome, very... exciting. Is that the word I want? I've agreed to go for a drive with him tomorrow, but I'm sorry that I did. He was a trifle too... flattering. I don't know..." Eleanor's voice died away.

"As long as he calls in an open carriage, there's nothing to concern yourself about. It will do you good to be seen with someone other than Jeremy. It doesn't pay to have one's name linked with one particular man, you know. You must have several admirers and treat them all equally if you don't wish to become an *on dit* for the *ton*." The eyes that were so like Geoffrey's closed as Lady Imogene let her head relax against the soft velvet squabs. "Did Geoffrey remark upon the comte's attentions?"

"No, of course not. Whyever should he? In fact, I haven't spoken to him for more than a moment since I danced with de Rochfort." Eleanor cast a suspicious look at her mother-in-law. "Why would you ask a question like that?"

"Oh, no reason, just wondering. What are you planning to wear for the rout tomorrow evening? And did you wish to accept Lady Winterset's invitation to her Venetian breakfast Tuesday next?"

A desultory conversation about their future engagements occupied the two women until they said their goodnights as they went up the staircase of Hellistone House. They parted at the head of the stairs and gave the other a goodnight kiss before entering their respective rooms. Eleanor closed the great door behind her and leaned against it, exhausted by the conflicting emotions she had experienced that evening. She would have to tread a fine line on the morrow lest de Rochfort take her polite amiability to mean more than just that. She wanted no further flattery or the protestations of abiding affection that she was sure would be forthcoming. Perhaps she should arrange to have her maid accompany them. That would tell him without words that she had no intention of dallying with him.

But all that could be decided tomorrow morning. Now she wanted only the oblivion of sleep, with perhaps dreams of a happier time with Geoffrey.

CHAPTER TEN

ELEANOR'S DREAMS WOULD have been nightmares had she overheard a conversation that took place between Alvinia and de Rochfort that night.

The French count was a regular visitor to Lady Coddington's boudoir, entering the house through a door hidden from passersby by the heavy shrubbery at the side of the house. Their connection was not known to the society in which they mingled, nor was it known that the comte was nothing more than a former secretary to a royal person who had died in penury many years before. In the same way that the so-called comte had stolen his employer's gold, he had stolen his name and proud lineage.

The man was a rake, an adventurer, and a thoroughgoing scoundrel, a suitable paramour for the blond jade. Their conversation that night boded no good for Eleanor.

"You seemed to have been well received by Lady de Maine, my love." Alvinia entwined her arms about her lover. "Did I hear you make a tryst with her?" She paused to enjoy his kisses. "I warn you though, you must keep your friendship very cool, or I shall take steps!"

"What kind of steps my blond enchantress? What does it matter to you what I do with her once I have her in my power? Do I question you when you tell me you are going to marry de Maine? We know each other too well to put up the fences. You like what I do to you, and you

know you wouldn't wish for me never to do this again."
His lips moved from her mouth to her neck as he began
to make passionate love to her.

For a long while there was the sound of sighs and
moans of ecstasy followed by flesh slapping against flesh
and then the high pitched cry of release. All was quiet
for a time, and then Alvinia reopened the conversation.

"When will you take her?"

"I plan to wind up this business by the end of next
week. I must wait until I hear from the captain of the
ship that will take her to France."

"I told you I wanted her gone by the end of *this* week!"
Alvinia sat up and pulled the coverlet around her naked
body. "And you must see that she never comes back.
What if she escapes? Have you thought about that? What
if she gets away from you before this captain and his
ship sail away from England?"

"Calm yourself, my dove. There will be no escape.
I have made a most careful plan." He pulled her down
next to him once more. "I will acquaint myself with her
habits and will win her trust. Tomorrow I take her driving. Lady de Maine will be surprised because I am sure
she will expect me to be very amorous. But I shall be
of the most polite, *le plus gentil*. Yes, she will come
with me willingly on the day that I shall choose to make
her disappear.

"The day after I take her driving," he continued, "I
shall send her the most discreet bouquet of flowers. Perhaps a few lilies with some forget-me-nots. Ah-h, I can
see her face now as she breathes in the scent. Then a
note on the following day requesting permission to pay
a morning call. I shall be charming, but still *pas d'amour*.
Instead, I shall have a problem that only she can help
me solve. I shall ask her to visit with me an elderly lady
who is ill, a former servant of my family now living just
outside London on the road to Brighton. Once she agrees,
we shall go in the closed carriage. If she insists on bring-

ing a maid, we shall have trouble with the coach and shall have to stop a while at one of the small inns on the way. Something will happen to make the maid very ill.

"Then we shall be ready for the grand finale. Once we are on the road, I shall offer the lady a restorative, a small cup of wine in which I will have placed a powder that will put her to sleep for some hours. When she wakes, she will be helpless and safely away from London and out of your life forever, my Alvinia! You see how well I have planned. Now you also must plan so that you have a busy schedule for the next week. I think it better if you deny yourself the pleasure of Lord Hellistone's company. Begin a wild flirtation with someone else so that attention will turn away from your dislike of the earl's wife. Soon, my pet, soon you will have all that lovely money for your own."

"It sounds wonderful. I know he will marry me once *she* is gone." Alvinia flung up her arms, reaching out in delight. "You are marvelous, my love. We shall have a wonderful time spending that huge fortune!"

Excited by the thought that she would have won her goal in the not-too-distant future, Alvinia made abandoned love to the man who was helping to attain that goal.

No matter how she tried to think of a way to gracefully decline de Rochfort's invitation the next morning, Eleanor could think of no excuse that would sound honest. It went against her grain to be deceitful, so she accepted her obligation in the same way she had accepted his invitation—with the hope that the hour would be a short one and, when it was over, she would be wise enough to refuse any further pleasures he might offer.

"Will you wear the teal-blue walking dress, my lady?" her maid asked. "The wine-colored gown is torn at the hem and the brown needs new buttons."

"Yes, the teal will do, Betty. Anything, anything."

Eleanor let the woman help her into the soft muslin dress and arrange her hair. "Betty, when I return to the house, if the comte should enter with me, I want you to tell Parkins to make sure he calls me away on a very urgent matter. Now get your bonnet and shawl. You'll be coming with us."

"But my lady, won't you be driving in one of them open carriages?"

"Yes, most likely. Why?"

"Well, there's hardly likely to be room for a third person, is there? I thought they were only big enough for two." The puzzled abigail waited for Eleanor's answer.

"You and I will take up no more room than one, and the other seat will be occupied by the comte." Eleanor looked at the woman. "I don't want to be alone with him, Betty. I don't really like him, and I wish I had never accepted his invitation. So you will go with me, and we shall take up no more room than one person."

Eleanor saw the dawn of understanding on Betty's face and was assured that there would be no untoward behavior on the part of the Frenchman as long as she was present.

Within the hour, Eleanor and the now-silent abigail were perched on the seat of the dashing midnight-blue curricle driven by an equally dashing man dressed in the height of fashion. His crisp linen, olive-green superfine jacket, tan buckskin pantaloons, and polished hessians were faultless. The several rings and fobs he wore as well as the oversized quizzing glass indicated leanings toward dandyism, but all told, he was an unexceptionable figure of a man.

To Eleanor's surprise, his manner reflected none of the amorous intent that she had sensed the previous evening. He was courteous, witty, and charming, although his charm seemed somewhat contrived. He accepted Betty's presence with a grave nod and proceeded to ignore her. He chatted lightly of the many *on dits* of the day, and Eleanor found herself carried away by laughter several times. When he suggested a stop at Gunther's for ices and insisted that Betty have her share, Eleanor found herself on the edge of liking the man, although the occasional glitter that seemed to flash in his eyes made her a trifle uneasy.

Despite that feeling, she had to admit that the drive was enjoyable. "Such a relief not to have to pretend deafness when one is toadied or lavished with unwanted attentions," she said to Mrs. Ogden upon her return. "He was quite pleasant, and I would have no qualms about accepting another invitation. I don't think he intended anything untoward. Perhaps I imagined his amatory inclinations. He might have dipped too deeply into that awful punch!"

"I'm sure I wouldn't know, love, but I cannot bring myself to like the man. The very fact that he is so much in Alvinia's pocket is enough to speak against him. Do be cautious with him. Not that I think he would do anything...nasty...but one never knows. After all, he is a Frenchman!" Mrs. Ogden felt like a Cassandra, warning of some vague ill-wind without being believed by her listeners.

"Dear Lucretia, I hope I am always cautious with any man," Eleanor replied. "I don't want any scenes of undying love. I'm afraid they would cast me into the whoops, and that would be too embarrassing for my would-be suitors." She picked at the dish of sliced tongue she had taken for lunch. "Do you think Geoffrey is..." Her voice died away in midquestion.

"Do I think Geoffrey is what, Eleanor?" Mrs. Ogden suspected the point of her companion's words, but refused to complete the sentence herself.

"Oh, nothing...just a silly wish. I think I must visit Madame Baleine this afternoon. I want to order a gown for the Venetian breakfast. I've had the most wonderful idea for something very different." Quickly, and with a pretense at enthusiasm, Eleanor described the dress she wished designed for her. Her gay manner and deliberate change of subject hid nothing from Mrs. Ogden. It was no news to the older woman that her beloved Eleanor was head-over-heels in love with the moody earl. If Mrs. Ogden had her way, she would have taken the two of them, shaken them vigorously, and then imprisoned them in some isolated spot until they had resolved their differences.

Not that the misunderstanding was entirely Eleanor's fault. The earl was being an impossible booby about his feelings for his wife. The man was mad about her and fighting his emotions every inch of the way. Carrying on with that blond light-skirt and who knew how many other women just to prove his independence, when any idiot could see the yearning on his face whenever he looked at Eleanor.

It was more than time that she took a hand in this comedy of errors. Lady Imogene had tried, but she was much too nice to do any really *serious* planning. After all, the dear lady had never had to run for her life and so had never developed the necessary attitudes for underhanded behavior. Perhaps that was why *this* old lady sensed something not quite right about that French comte. Probably no more a count than she was a countess! It was about time to consult Mr. Ferret. He would get to the bottom of things.

Once having decided on a plan of action, Mrs. Ogden settled back to her luncheon, delicately slicing a piece of meat from the plump breast of chicken on her plate. "What color were you thinking of ordering, my dear?" she asked, picking up the conversation concerning Eleanor's about-to-be ordered dress. "You haven't had anything in coral for quite some time. Very good on you . . . perhaps with lace inserts?"

* * *

Two hours later Mrs. Ogden was wending her way to the lawyer's office. Once announced, she was received with flattering speed.

"My dear Lucretia, it's been quite some time since you've graced my humble office with your presence. How have you been?" Mr. Ferret gently led the white-haired lady to a tall-backed arm-chair and took her parasol, shawl, reticule, and package while she seated herself.

"As always, Adolphus, as always. Hale and hearty. And yourself? You do look well, I must say. How's your lovely wife? It's been too long, old friend."

"We go along quite peaceably these days, Lucretia. Jane is away attending our daughter-in-law, who expects her first child momentarily. Can you imagine, I'm to be a grandfather! When I think of the harum-scarum lad whom you befriended and whom Miss Shappley saw through the study of the law . . . well! It seems like centuries ago."

"Yes . . . well . . . It's all very good to reminisce, Adolphus, but I have no time for that now. I've come on serious business." Mrs. Ogden settled herself more comfortably before she began her tale. "It's my dear Eleanor, Adolphus. I think she's gotten herself into an involvement . . . well, not really an involvement, more like a brush with a character I think is rather unsavory. So-called Comte de Rochfort. Alvinia Coddington has him riding on her skirts and introduced him to Linnet. Nasty piece, she is. Can't imagine that she'd be so cozy with any right'un. If she were, she'd take care not to let any other female get wind of him! You know her, and she gives nothing away!"

Mr. Ferret leaned back in his oversized chair, steepling his hands under his chin as he considered Mrs.

Ogden's words. "You make some sense there, Lucretia. But what makes you think this man is aimed at Eleanor? It could be nothing more than an acquaintanceship."

"Oh, no, not that one. He does nothing without a reason, and I have a feeling in my bones that the reason has to do with Eleanor's marriage to Geoffrey. That yellow-haired mockery of a woman would like nothing better than to have the earl in her pocket once more. She knows he's all Eleanor's, for all he's fighting the feeling, and she's livid with it. It wouldn't surprise me at all to know that she and that French dandy of hers have planned some mischief for my girl between them. I want you to find out all you can about that man, Adolphus, and watch over Eleanor. You have the means to find out what you have to, and you owe it to Miss Shappley, for all she's done these years. She did love Eleanor and Phillip . . . did all she could for them, including putting you in charge of her fortune. Now, earn your money." Mrs. Ogden emphasized her words with a sharp slap at the arm of her chair.

"Are you telling me you expect this de Rochfort to harm Eleanor in some way?"

"How should I know? But with Alvinia writing the score, I wouldn't discount anything."

"If that's the case, I shall have to take steps to protect our Eleanor . . . Hmmm." He paused a moment in thought, then said, "All right, Lucretia, you may leave everything safely to me. I'll look into this man's background and see that Eleanor is protected. Do see what you can do to caution her so that she's not too quick to accept his company again."

"I knew I could count on you, Adolphus. You're made of good stuff." Mrs. Ogden hauled herself to her feet and located her various belongings. "There's no sense in making a big to-do over this with Lady Imogene and her son—at least not yet. Immy will only get angry, and the earl will ridicule the whole thing. Best to let it lay quiet

until you come up with something." She accepted her
parasol and a helping hand from her friend.

"Think you're right about that," Mr. Ferret agreed.
"People don't like to believe what they don't want to.
And from what you tell me, the earl has a touch too
much pride to take kindly to anyone saying his 'friend'
would do something underhanded about the countess.
You let me take care of things first. We'll see what we
can do without coming out about it all."

Feeling much more at ease now that she had an ally,
Mrs. Ogden took leave of Mr. Ferret and returned to
Hellistone House to dress for the evening. With luck,
she would see that the next act of this little entertainment
would have the benefit of her direction.

CHAPTER ELEVEN

ELEANOR, AS USUAL, had great success at the rout that evening. She was acclaimed as an Incomparable, a gem of the first water. The elderly dowagers complimented Lady Imogene on her daughter-in-law's manners. "Don't take herself too seriously. Not full of herself like some I could name," was one lady's comment.

The gentlemen also appreciated her charm and wit, and the younger of them applauded her serious attention when spoken to about those subjects so dear to their hearts—Mr. Jackson's parlor and the great whipsters of the time as well as the more exciting facets of the newest craze, hot-air balloons. One nineteen-year-old, who was making his first appearance in Society, was heard to compare the lady to his favorite horse. "Throws her heart over the fence without care or caution." Fortunately, his elder brother took care to enlighten him on the folly of bandying about a lady's name, and few people heard his encomium.

To Eleanor's great relief and secret sorrow, Geoffrey did not accompany them to the rout. He excused himself, pleading a prior engagement at White's. It was quite demeaning to Eleanor to think that her husband preferred an evening of gambling to her company, but she had come to expect no more from him and was able to console herself by vowing to enjoy her evening as much as possible.

Further, to Eleanor's surprise, Alvinia was present at the event, once more accompanied by the Comte de Rochfort. The earl's former fiancée made certain to speak to Eleanor during the course of the evening. Her manner was almost cordial as she greeted Eleanor and brought the comte to her attention again.

A fringe of dark eyelashes dropped over Eleanor's hazel eyes before the comte could see the flash of discomfort in them. To her relief, the Frenchman remained aloof from the proceedings, merely acknowledging Eleanor with a courteous bow. After a few moments of light conversation, Alvinia and de Rochfort moved on.

"Why didn't you say anything . . . or make an assignation with her?" Lady Coddington hissed.

"Let me do this my way. She will not respond to the invitation to dally. She is in love with her husband even though he hurts her. No, we will stick to our plan. She is more apt to respond to a request for help than to take a lover." De Rochfort's eyes lingered on the subject of his talk. He would enjoy that woman. Oh, to be sure, he would enjoy her.

The following day, after a sleepless night, Eleanor decided that she had had enough of the *haut monde* for the time being. Without giving much thought to her plan, she betook herself to Lady Imogene's room to present the idea to her as a *fait accompli*.

"I hate to leave Town in the midst of all these wonderful entertainments," she said, "and knowing how hard you've worked to have me accepted by all your friends, but my man in Brighton has written to me that a problem requires my attention. The house Miss Shappley left me is part of a row of houses in Brunswick Square—actually in Hove—and there seems to have been a fire in the one next to mine that has caused some damage. He wants me to glance at his choices for refurbishing the rooms and give my signature—one of those bothersome details that are so necessary."

"Yes, quite," the dowager countess agreed dryly. "I know excuses when I hear them, my girl. I've made enough of them myself. Now, what maggot's got into your brain that has you running away from London in the middle of the season?"

"You know me too well, Belle-mère," Eleanor acknowledged with a laugh. "It's no maggot. I'm just exhausted from all the frivolity. You don't mind that I want to go off by myself for a few days, do you? I have a need to refresh myself. But please, don't tell anyone why I've gone. I'm sure no one will really care."

"For 'no one' you mean Geoffrey?" Shrewd eyes watched for telltale signs. "I don't know where he got his pigheadedness! Certainly not from *my* side of the family. Do you think Phillip has inherited it? I hope not. Go, by all means. You'll feel better for a short stay away from the fleshpots of the city. When do you mean to leave?"

"It will take much of the day for Betty to go through my clothes and pack a bag, and I have an appointment to go riding with young Venner this morning." She smiled when her mother-in-law grimaced. "I know, he's a bit of a bore, but he's so young. I couldn't bring myself to squelch his pretensions to being a man of the world. And who knows, perhaps he will be so puffed up with his own consequence as a result of riding out with the Countess Hellistone that *he* will become the male version of the belle of the ball!

"In any case," she continued, "I plan on leaving tomorrow, about noon. If I take my time I can make it easily in a few hours. 'Tis no more than fifty miles. Even if I should make a stop for a nuncheon, I shall still arrive before dark. And I'll have Betty with me and probably Parkins's son, Jamie, and maybe one other to carry a brace of pistols. It's a well-traveled road, so there's really no reason to fear any foul play."

"And how long shall you stay?"

"In all likelihood I'll be back for the Venetian break-fast—that's Tuesday, isn't it? That will give me a good three days for myself and one day going and one coming. Five days in all, or four-and-a-half if I leave Hove early in the day and arrive back here in the early afternoon." She smiled at Lady Imogene. "I feel quite the truant! Why aren't you trying to dissuade me?"

"I wouldn't dream of it. You've been looking a bit fagged. It will do you a world of good to be by yourself for a while. Will you be making an early night of it tonight, or may I look forward to your joining me for the theater?"

"May I tell you later? I haven't decided whether it would be better to be seen as the scintillating Lady de Maine this evening or more appealing to put it about that I've gone into a slight decline and must withdraw for my health. What do you recommend?"

"Me? I recommend that you stop bamming me and go on about your business! Whatever you decide will be fine, my love. Just make sure you bid me good-bye before you take your leave tomorrow."

While Eleanor made plans to escape to Hove for a few days' holiday, Geoffrey was recovering from a night on the tiles. He had gambled until the early hours of the morning, overindulged in brandy, and wound up in the arms of a pretty little piece who had come to town with the new opera company. To his half-remembered dis-tress, his ladybird had been displeased with his perfor-mance when he left her near dawn. She had complained that he had been more interested in sleep than in her charms and had offered her the grossest insult by ad-dressing her as Linnet each time she had kissed him. His temper was, to say the least, on the verge of violence.

It took no more than the news that his wife was taking a short trip away from the town environs to set match to the tinder. In a stentorian roar, the earl announced his displeasure, unaware that he was informing the whole household except for his wife, who had taken herself off to keep her appointment with young Venner.

"Geoffrey, my dear, what's happened? Did you injure yourself?" Lady Imogene had come running to the scene of expected mayhem, dreading the bloodshed she was sure she would find. "Is anyone hurt? Tell me, please. What's wrong?"

"Wrong? What's wrong? Just that my wife is removing herself in the middle of the season that she was so impatient to enjoy. That's what's wrong!" The usually subtle tones of the earl's velvety voice were rasping with wrath.

"My dear boy, stop making a cake of yourself. You must have indulged yourself a trifle too well last night. Do you realize you're advertising your excesses to the whole household?" Lady Imogene's calm tone gradually attracted the earl's attention. "Much better, son, not to bellow. One can hear what you have to say more easily. If you would seat yourself in your anteroom, Burton will bring you a posset that will make you feel more yourself." She gently urged her son into a large, comfortable armchair and pushed an ottoman beneath his feet. "That's right, now lift your legs and stretch them out on the footstool. That's the boy..."

"All right, Mother. I shall apologize most abjectly if you will only stop talking to me as though I were a child."

"As long as you stop acting like a child, my dear, you will receive the treatment you desire." Lady Imogene waved the valet into the room and gave him instructions on preparing a potion for the earl. Burton nodded twice and quickly left to fill her order. "In just a trice, my dear, you'll be feeling all of a piece. While we wait, perhaps you'd care to tell me what you were bellowing about."

"I wasn't bellowing!" At the sight of her raised eyebrows and half smile, Geoffrey's mouth curled in a penitent grin. "I must have gotten up on the wrong side of the bed, and my head was . . . *is* . . . banging rather dreadfully. Am I forgiven?"

"Of course, dearest. Now, what were you bruiting so noisily about?"

"What's this I hear about Eleanor going to Hove tomorrow?"

"Oh that. Yes, the dear girl had a message from her man down there that some matters needed her immediate personal attention. She's also a bit fagged from all the gadding about—not used to it, y'know—so I told her I thought it would be a fine idea for her to take a little rest."

"Ummm. I hadn't noticed."

"Well, you haven't seen very much of her lately." Geoffrey's mother idly inspected her neatly buffed fingernails. "Not much of a way to conduct a marriage, if you ask me."

"Well, I'm not asking you, Mama dear, so don't interfere." The earl sat brooding, waiting for his valet to return with the medication his mother had asked for. "It's a problem, Mother, a problem."

"There's a simple solution, you know."

"She doesn't want me, though. I think I'll have to . . . Ah, here's Burton." He downed the glass of whitish liquid in one swallow. "Ugh! What's in that? Horrible!"

"You'll be blessing it shortly, Geoffrey. Since you don't wish to discuss your problem, I'll leave you to your dressing. Shall you see Eleanor before she leaves?"

"I don't know. Perhaps."

"Foolish boy!" Lady Imogene left her son in a huff. She hoped Eleanor's action might jolt the fool out of whatever hidey-hole he was in. His refusal to admit his love for his wife was the most exasperating nonsense Lady Imogene could remember having to contend with. And that it should be her own son! Well!

Geoffrey had almost recovered from the terrible headache that had bothered him all morning when Parkins entered his room to announce that Lady de Maine's man of business had arrived and begged the favor of an interview with Lord de Maine.

"Tell him I'll be with him in a few moments, Parkins. You can put him in the blue salon, and don't forget the claret. He'll be thirsty, I'm sure." At the butler's look of reproach, he continued, "I know I don't have to remind you—force of habit. Sorry. When I am closeted with him, make sure we remain private. I'll ring if we need anything."

The earl straightened his cravat and donned a russet kerseymere jacket with bone buttons that matched his drill riding trousers. He flicked his handkerchief at his white-topped boots, slid his signet ring over his knuckle, and gave a final twitch to his lapels before leaving the room. As he ran lightly down the staircase and entered the room where Mr. Ferret was comfortably esconced, he wondered what Eleanor's man of business could want with him.

"My lord, so kind of you to see me." The attorney bowed.

"Not at all, Ferret, not at all. Good to see you. Are you sure you wanted to see me and not m'wife?"

"Quite certain, my lord. In fact, I came about Lady de Maine." The lawyer rose and paced restlessly about the room. He rubbed his hand over his clean-shaven face, coughed once or twice to clear his throat, and gestured with his hands as though accenting words he was speaking to himself. Finally he cleared his throat a last time, poured himself another glass of wine, and sat down knee-to-knee with the earl.

"My lord." Still he hesitated. "My lord," he began again. "My lord, you know that I am deeply concerned in you wife's affairs. *Business affairs.* Well . . . harrumph . . . Sir . . . Demme, but this is more difficult than I thought it would be."

"Speak out, man. What's bothering you? No round-aboutation, straight talk," the earl exhorted him.

"Very well. I've known Linnet for seven years, and she's been like a daughter to me. Her benefactress and my wife had been friends for many years. When Miss Shappley adopted Eleanor, I became her substitute father. Miss Shappley felt it unwise to bring a young woman to maturity without a man in the picture. Of course Linnet was eighteen or more, but she was very young for her age. Har-r-umph . . . Well! To continue, I was given the task by Miss Shappley of watching over Eleanor. We didn't know whether she would ever find the father of her child, and arrangements would have to be made for the little one, and if she wanted to marry again . . . and all the various difficulties that could crop up . . . I don't have to spell it out for you. Anyway, my lord—"

"Oh for God's sake man, call me Geoffrey and be done with it. If you call my wife Linnet, how can you keep 'my lording' me?"

"H-mmm, yes, well thank you my . . . Geoffrey. Where was I? Oh, yes. Well. I've noticed that Linnet hasn't been so happy since she's come to London. Wondered why and she told me you two don't seem to be getting on too well. That you seem to prefer the life of a bachelor to that of a wedded man. Eh? Told her things would work out. I hope I was right? But in any case, that's not the only reason I've come. The other thing is, Mrs. Ogden told me about this de Rochfort man. Says he was dangling after Eleanor and didn't like it one bit. Did a little looking into it and the man's a bounder, sir. A bounder!"

"I'm aware of that," the earl replied. "I've been trying to watch after her myself."

"Good, good. Then I take it you *do* have Linnet's best interests at heart?"

"Of course. No need to ask that." Geoffrey's indignant expression turned thoughtful. His behavior the past several weeks would indicate otherwise. "Well, perhaps you did have to ask. Judging by my actions lately, one might not know that I care for Eleanor. Suppose I ought to tell her." He gazed at Mr. Ferret, who was smiling broadly now that his fears had been allayed. "Beg your forgiveness, sir . . . must find my wife." He left the room quickly, almost bumping into Mrs. Ogden as he went.

"What have you done to his lordship, Adolphus?" she asked, sailing into the room. "He seemed in quite a hurry."

"Yes . . . well . . . I believe he's gone to find his countess to straighten out certain things with her. I do believe I've done a good day's work here, Lucretia. A good day's work."

"Did you tell him you're having de Rochfort followed?"

"No, why upset the man more than he is? He's going to have to convince Linnet that he's a changed man. He's been rightly caught in parson's mousetrap now, and I do believe he'll like every minute of it."

The two friends laughed together, enjoying the thought that their dear Linnet would be all the happier for the change in her husband.

Unfortunately, the husband who had changed was having no luck in finding his wife. She had returned from her riding engagement with Venner and, after changing, had left the house once more to accomplish certain errands. The rest of the day was a frustrating series of events in which the earl kept missing his wife. On finding that she had left, he went out to try to find her, thinking that she might possibly have gone to Bond Street to the jewelers. He wandered the length of the short road, then returned to Hellistone House to find that Eleanor had been and gone again. This time she was engaged to visit a Lady Thomas, with whom Geoffrey was unfamiliar. The coachman didn't know her direction because Lady de Maine had taken her curricle and her abigail and groom with her and none had as yet returned.

Then Geoffrey had to leave. He had sent a note to Alvinia begging her indulgence that evening. He wanted to inform her that he could no longer be considered one of her beaux. He was retiring to the country with his wife and son, and she should no longer count on his supportive presence. Of course, he would make her a generous gift . . . but that would be the end of it.

By sheer mischance, Eleanor overheard Parkins mention my lord's engagement. Not knowing this was to be his last visit to the demimondaine, she became furious at Geoffrey's further blatant disregard for their marriage. She was more than ever convinced that she must untie the nuptial knot, and she closeted herself in her room for the rest of the day with instructions that she was in to no one—not Lady Imogene, Mrs. Ogden, or her husband. She busied herself with sorting through some of the mementos of her London visit and shed a few tears over a flower saved from a bouquet the earl had sent her. As she sat over the dried bud, she came across a note from de Rochfort asking her to ride with him the day after next.

She had completely forgotten that she had accepted his invitation! Quickly she called Betty to her and wrote a note of regret as she directed the girl to deliver it to the comte. "Be sure he gets it, Betty. I wouldn't want to insult him by having him arrive here only to find me away."

"Yes, ma'am, I'll be sure."

"And Betty, tell Parkins that I want the coach for ten in the morning. I've decided to leave earlier than I had originally planned. We'll stop for a nuncheon at the Grey Gull in Reigate. He'll have to send a postboy on to Horsham for a change of horses. Please remind him of it."

"Yes, my lady. Oh, I'm that excited, my lady. I've never been to Brighton. Shall we see the Royal Pavilion there? I've heard it's ever so unusual."

"Perhaps. We'll see how busy we are. Now, go along. It's getting late."

The maid disappeared, willing to run the errand for her mistress. Mistakenly the girl believed she was running in love's cause. She knew there was friction in the household and felt sorry for her beautiful mistress. She also knew it was common among the upper classes for married couples to make liaisons outside of the marriage.

When she arrived at the comte's narrow rowhouse on the edge of Kensington Gardens, she was able to deliver the note into the hands of the dark-visaged Frenchman himself. He perused it quickly, muttering an oath under his breath.

"When does the countess depart for this place?" he asked the maid.

"She told me to ask the butler to order the carriage for ten, sir."

"And what road does she take?"

"I dunno . . . she didn't tell me." Betty looked inquiringly at him. "I don't think I should be telling you this."

"Don't be stupid, girl. Your mistress would want me to know." He stood a moment, thinking. He could not allow her to escape him this way. How to take her tomorrow? Suddenly his face cleared. "Where does she plan to stop, do you know?"

"She said something about the Grey Gull . . . in Reigate I think it was." When she saw the smile on the comte's face, Betty decided she was really helping the cause of love. She wouldn't tell the countess; she'd have to scold her for giving out the information even if she truly wanted her gallant to know her plans.

"Don't tell my lady," the comte cautioned as he handed the girl a shilling. "Perhaps I can surprise her."

"Oh sir, that would be so . . . so . . . fanciful. I'm sure she'd like it. You can count on me not to say a word."

The door closed behind the unsuspecting abigail, who went happily on her way. Before she had passed from sight, de Rochfort was issuing orders to his man, calling for his closed carriage and pair to be ready at dawn. He rapidly wrote two missives and instructed a groom to see to their delivery; one to go to a small inn in Shoreham and one to the captain of the boat he kept there. He would take Eleanor when she stopped at the inn in Reigate. And the beauty of it was no one would miss her for several days. Plenty of time to dally and then get her aboard the boat for a quick trip to France. Once she had been with him for a few days, she'd never look to return to her life in England. And she had her own money! She would deliver him from this life of running after Alvinia!

CHAPTER TWELVE

ELEANOR HAD BEEN gone from Hellistone House for more than two hours the following day when Mr. Ferret drove up in a hackney. Commanding the driver to await his return, he ran up the steps to the imposing front door and used the knocker vigorously, shouting for someone to open up immediately. Just as he was about to use his fist on the wood panels, the door flew wide, and the startled butler looked out at him.

"Quickly," Mr. Ferret said, "conduct me to the earl. I have very important news for him."

"I beg your pardon sir, the earl is not yet dressed."

"I don't care if he's in his bath! Take me to him, man. There's serious mischief afoot." He started up the stairway, not waiting for Parkins. "I'll find him myself. Where's his room?"

"Sir, sir . . . Just a minute—you can't . . ." The frantic words were trailing from his mouth when he observed the earl at the head of the stairs. "My lord . . ."

Mr. Ferret sighed with relief at the sight of Eleanor's husband, dressed and ready for the street. "Thank goodness you're here," he said. "De Rochfort's on his way. Has Eleanor left?"

"Parkins? Has Lady de Maine left for Brighton?" Geoffrey asked the butler.

"Yes sir, she was gone by ten o'clock. She came out of Lady Imogene's room and left directly."

"Did she take anyone with her?" Mr. Ferret demanded.

"Of course, sir. Betty and my son accompanied her. My son drove the carriage, and Ned Bristol rode her horse. It's a busy road sir. Nothing can happen to her."

"In the normal course of events, Parkins, I would say you are quite right," Mr. Ferret said. "But we have a villainous action planned here and needs must be on our way before it's too late."

"How do you know de Rochfort is following Eleanor?" Geoffrey queried. "He could be on his way to keep any kind of appointment?"

"My men have been following him these last three days. I expected him to try something. That lady friend of yours was getting anxious about the continuation of your relationship with her, and she's as close as a bed sheet to our friend, the Frenchman." Mr. Ferret walked down the steps as he spoke. "I have a hackney outside. I'll pay him while you get ready. Since your wife already has a carriage, I think we should ride. Much faster that way. Can you mount me, Geoffrey?"

"Yes, of course. Parkins, have Bob saddle up Major and Taffy. And get my travel bag from my room. And I'll need money from the safe and my guns. Adolphus, I'll be with you in a trice."

At the moment that Mr. Ferret was informing the Earl of de Rochfort's actions, Eleanor's driver was pulling into the yard of the Grey Gull posting house. The countess dismounted from the vehicle, aided by the waiting landlord, who greeted her arrival with the news that a private parlor awaited her and a pretty nuncheon would be served as soon as she had refreshed herself.

Thanking the innkeeper, Eleanor bade her maid to follow and directed her two men servants to take themselves to the kitchens for refreshments, telling them that she would be ready in two hours to continue on to Brighton.

The room to which she was shown was comfortably furnished with a dining table and chairs, several armchairs, and a settle. Hanging from the brick facing around a large hearth were the usual fireplace implements as well as several long-handled finjeans for heating wine or other potables.

"This will do very nicely," Eleanor commented to the host as she removed her straw bonnet. "If you could have a ewer of water and a bowl brought in so I may wash my hands?"

"Certainly, my lady. I have had a nice spring lamb roasted as well as a pair of pullets, tender as anything, and I thought perhaps some young peas and a few garden greens? Also a syllabub and some fresh-picked strawberries, just off the vine."

"That sounds lovely, landlord. I believe I'll do it justice, for I am famished. Betty, you may stay and eat with me or join Ned and Jem in the kitchen. Which do you prefer?"

The abigail blushed slightly and hung her head. "If you wouldn't mind, my lady, Jem and me, we have an understanding, and I would dearly love to sit with him awhile."

"Take a towel out of my box and my bottle of eau de cologne and then you may run along." Eleanor smiled at the young maid. "You won't have to hurry. If we leave by half after two, there'll be time enough to reach Hove before dusk."

"Oh, thank you, my lady. Thank you." The young woman rummaged through the packed container for the requested items, then helped Eleanor straighten her hair and clothes. Once she was satisfied that her lady no longer needed her attention, Betty headed for the kitchen and her young man.

Shortly after she had gone, a light tap on the door received Eleanor's word to enter. She was standing at the window with her back to the room watching the busy hostlers working in the yard. She turned, startled, when a familiar voice said, "My Lady de Maine, what wondrous accident of fate brought you to this hostelry?" The Comte de Rochfort stood with his hand on the doorknob, eyeing Eleanor with a most repulsive leer. "May I join you?" Without waiting for her permission, he entered the chamber and closed the door carefully behind him.

"How came you here, sir?" Eleanor inquired warily. "I had not expected to see you again until I returned to London next week."

"I received an unlooked-for request for aid from an old family retainer. She is in a bad way and has no one to turn to but myself. Oddly enough, she lives on the outskirts of Hove, in Shoreham. I cannot believe my good fortune to have been here when you arrived."

De Rochfort's company was the last thing Eleanor wanted. But how to get out of this uncomfortable situation without insulting the man?

"Yes, very fortunate, indeed," she agreed. "But perhaps, since the woman's case is so desperate, you will want to hurry on. I plan to rest here for quite a while. Travel wearies me so." As does the company of those I don't wish to be with, she added silently to herself.

"No, no, an hour or two will make no difference. Are you awaiting your *déjeuner?* You would not object if I joined you? *Bien.* To have the opportunity to spend a time with so beautiful a lady as yourself is not to be ignored, *n'est-ce pas?* Ah, here is the landlord with the trays." The aggravating man opened the door for the parade of tray-carrying servants, who quickly set the table and distributed their dishes upon it. Before Eleanor had a chance to request that her maid be sent to her, the comte had ushered them out of the room and returned to her. "May I seat you, madame?" he asked as he pulled a chair away from the table.

"This is most improper, sir," Eleanor protested. "I would like to have my maid here." She made a movement toward the bellpull.

"I must refuse you this so little desire, my lady. We have things to speak of which would better be unheard by a gossiping servant." The fulsome voice had an underlying edge to it that put Eleanor on her guard. "Come, let us break bread together. Better to be... what is the word... *être a l'aise,* comfortable than to be enemies."

The countess seated herself coolly. "I don't like to be constrained or compromised sir, but I agree, it is better to act in a civilized manner." She began to help herself to the assorted foods before her. "What is it you wish to speak to me about?"

"Later we will talk business. For now let us be two friends who have met by chance and wish only to speak of things mutually entertaining. Did you visit Ranelagh this past week?"

Feeling as though she had stepped onto the stage of a theater, Eleanor maintained a light social attitude. She smiled occasionally, offered opinions on art, music, and literature when asked a direct question, and endeavored to understand what coil the comte had woven. That it had something to do with Alvinia, she had no doubt. That he was not interested in Eleanor's future happiness was also in no doubt. Whether she should be frightened was questionable. She had dealt with a villain once before. Hopefully she would be able to deal with whatever fate this one had in store for her.

The hour passed pleasantly enough, if one discounted the shade of fear that Eleanor could not push aside. At last they had finished eating, had used the proffered fingerbowls and cloths, and had moved away from the table. Eleanor refilled her wineglass before seating herself on the stiff settle to await the comte's declaration of his intent.

"The time has come for us to depart, *chère madame*. We go to Shoreham, as I have told you, but from there we will travel to France. I wish to show you the beauties of my country... and to enjoy your beauty at the same time. You will not fight with me. There is nothing you can do about it."

The comte's words brought Eleanor to her feet. "You must be mad, m'sieu," she declared. "I have three servants with me, none of whom will permit you to take me away without an outcry."

"Ah, but they will know nothing about it. Even now they are busy taking their ease and have no thought that you might have need of them yet. You will notice that you are beginning to feel a trifle light-headed. Soon you will fall asleep. I put a powder in your wine when you were unaware of my movements. So much less noisy that way." His hawk eyes watched as she lifted a hand to her brow, feeling a muzziness cloud her brain.

"You'll never... never... get... away w-w-ith this..." Eleanor could feel her knees weakening as a cloud of darkness seemed to descend upon her head. "Geo..." She slumped into unconsciousness, caught by the comte, who leaped to her side before she could fall to the floor.

"Ah, so well done. She is a true beauty. Life will be very enjoyable for a while." He laid her on the settle and went to the window, pushing the mullioned panel outward. "Pierre, Pierre," he called to one of his men, *"viens-ici. J'ai la comtesse.* Take her from me through the window. Good, now place her in the carriage before you are seen. *Bien."*

As soon as he had lifted the unconscious form through the opening, the comte moved back into the room to find Eleanor's bonnet and appurtenances. When he had finished, there was no indication that the countess had ever been there, other than the soiled dishes. These the comte piled on a tray and cautiously, making sure there were no witnesses, placed on a table in the hall. He stepped back into the room, quietly closed the door, and locked it. Once more he went to the window, this time climbing through and pushing it closed from the outside.

"Now," he said to his coachman as he climbed on the box, "let us be off. I do not expect any pursuit, but there's no reason to waste time in any case. I have a lovely evening planned for my guest and myself."

As the black coach pulled out of the inn's yard, a figure on horseback watched. He gave a soft whistle, calling the attention of another man, and indicated the direction the coach had taken. "I'll be follerin' it. Do you tell someone that we're on the road. One of us will leave word if he don't keep to the highroad. Hurry along then." With those instructions, he touched his mount lightly with his spur and was off on the trail of his quarry.

The second man, one of two trusted servants set to watch the comte by Mr. Ferret, went round to the back of the inn to warn the de Maine servants of the departure of the countess and her abductor. Asking them to give a history of the events they had seen to Mr. Ferret and the earl, both of whom would be hot on the trail, he returned to his horse, remounted, and took off after his partner.

When the carriage had reached Horsham, the two watchdogs had met up again. They were able to leave a message with the head groom of the posting house where the earl kept a pair of horses. Just before reaching the final miles to Hove, the comte turned off onto a side road that led to Shoreham. One of the men waited at the roadsign for those he knew were following.

Eleanor was just coming out of her swoon when the carriage arrived at a tumbledown cottage on the edge of a deserted stretch of beach. The comte shook her awake and urged her out of the coach. "Take it back to the road and on to Brighton. Then stable the horses and disappear.

We leave for France on the early tide tomorrow."

A consuming tide of hopelessness swept over Eleanor at the sound of the man's words. "No . . . you can't . . . what do you want? Why are you doing this?" she cried. "You must be mad to think you can get away with this."

A hard smile crossed the Frenchman's face. "You know I can succeed. No one will have missed you at the inn until well after we left. By the time one of them returns to London to alert your family it will be evening. By the time they trace us here—*if* they do—we shall be long gone. I planned everything with great care, my dear Eleanor. You don't mind if I call you that, do you? We are going to be great friends, you and I. Now, if you will enter this little abode, we'll spend the night here— in mutual enjoyment, I hope."

As the man spoke, Eleanor's courage returned. He might be very sure of himself, but there was no putting *finis* to the story until it was well and truly over. She walked silently through the shabby garden into the house, where a few scattered pieces of broken furniture offered one a precarious perch if one chose to sit. Eleanor chose one that looked in fair repair and dusted it with her gloves, then seated herself. The Frenchman watched her, amazed at her sangfroid in the face of such a situation.

Controlling her voice, she once more asked his reason for such an action. "I could understand you if you were to ask for a ransom. My husband is a very wealthy man. But to take me to France?"

"You appeal to me, madame. You have a certain *je ne sais quoi,* an inner fire that I like. Alvinia wanted me to kill you, but that would be such a waste. This way, we can live together and love together and possibly stay together if all goes well. If not . . . well, there are many men who would pay to have you."

"Pay to have me!" Horror tore through her breast. How low could this man be to even contemplate selling her.

She must remain cool. She would need every scrap of courage she'd ever had to get out of this. If not... what was the old saying? Death before dishonor.

"You don't paint a very rosy future for me, m'sieu," she said calmly. "You are aware that I am a wealthy woman in my own right? I could pay you to buy myself from you. Had you thought of that?"

"It had crossed my mind, dear lady, but I would rather spend the money and have you at the same time. That way I have the best of both."

"You are despicable." Eleanor's voice was dispassionate, measuring. "Do you expect me to submit without a fight?"

"When you realize that anything you are hoping for is not going to come to pass, you will welcome my loving arms. You are a passionate woman, Eleanor. I see it in your eyes and in your body. You are a married woman. How long before you will want me? I am not so horrible in my physical attributes that you will be able to shun me forever. Naturally, I would rather have you willingly. But if not..." He shrugged.

She moved in her chair, turning away from him as though to ponder his words, but studying the room instead, looking for a possible weapon to use against him. Thank goodness he had sent his men away. At least she would not have to worry about them.

A poker was lying half-in and half-out of the fireplace, and an iron frying pan lay under the table in the corner. If she could move about the room without arousing his suspicions, she might have a chance to get the one or the other.

"Do you have anything to offer to drink," she asked, "or does your hospitality consist only of threats, sir?" Perhaps he would leave the room to fetch some wine or water.

"Of course we can offer you wine, madame. And if you are hungry, a bit of bread and cheese. As soon as I lock the door so that you don't go flying out when I leave the room, I shall bring you some refreshment. I am glad you have decided to be sensible about this. Much more the thing." Trailing a laugh of triumph at what he took to be his captive's capitulation, the comte left the room.

Eleanor ran quickly to the fireplace and grabbed the long iron rod. She moved to the table and stooped to pick up the frying pan. The best time to mount her attack would be when he returned from the kitchen or pantry with his hands full. If she were to stand close to the doorway, she would be able to hit him with the pan and hold him at bay with the poker. Hopefully her arm was strong enough so that her blow would level him, in which case she could tear her petticoat into strips to tie him up.

The sound of her heart pounding with fear and excitement obscured the pounding of hooves racing down the path to the cottage. De Rochfort's voice, raised in song, came to her through the wall, getting closer and closer. She pressed herself into the shadow at the side of the door, waiting for him to enter. Perspiration trickled down her back between her shoulder blades, and she hoped there was no smell of fear about her to warn him.

"Here you are, *chérie,* a magnificent wine for a magnificent woman." His voice seemed to boom through the small room. He stepped through the doorway. "Where did you—"

His words were cut off when the heavy iron pan connected with his skull with a loud thud. As if in slow motion, the tray dropped from his hands, the bottle and glasses slid from the falling tray, and everything hit the floor sending shattered glass and drops of crimson wine bouncing upward. The comte's body seemed to fold up as he fell, a look of complete surprise on his face. His head hit the stone floor with a loud thud.

Eleanor stood away from the fallen man, holding the poker at the ready should he move. Shocked by what she'd accomplished, she realized she hadn't planned her next step.

When Geoffrey came crashing through the locked door moments later, the picture he saw before him became emblazoned in his mind. His elegant wife, not a hair out of place, stood looking at de Rochfort, who was laid low on the floor, with a look of mingled satisfaction, loathing, and horror on her face, holding the long iron poker as though it were a sword she was about to thrust through the supine man.

"Eleanor, darling, thank God we found you in time." Geoffrey ran to her side, wanting to enfold her in his arms.

"Get away from me you—you traitor! Don't you dare touch me!" she screamed at him, threatening him with her weapon. "I don't want to have anything to do with you. If it hadn't been for your idiotic behavior with that wretch Alvinia, Lady Codface, I would never have been in this fix. Go away!" She stamped her foot, enraged. "Go *away!*"

Unseen by either party, Mr. Ferret had entered the room in time to hear Eleanor's denunciation of her husband. Slowly, the elderly gentleman walked to the distraught woman's side, took the poker from her hands, and put his arms around her. "There, there, you've had a very upsetting day. Come along now. We've brought your carriage and Betty, and you'll be all settled down in no time." Keeping his voice a soothing flow, he nodded to Geoffrey, mouthing a caution at him, then led Eleanor from the room. Not until she was ensconced in her coach with Betty's warm arms holding her in comfort did she break down in tears.

"Now, now, my lady, everything's going to be all right. We'll be in Brighton in no time at all and then it's a nice warm bath for you and some sleep. You'll feel better as soon as you've had your rest."

Under the ministrations of the devoted abigail, Eleanor's sobbing tapered off. By the time the carriage reached Brunswick Square, Eleanor was almost herself.

"I suppose I shall have to invite you in," she said grudgingly to her spouse when he presented himself at the side of the carriage. "You may come in, at least until your man can find you quarters elsewhere." A pang reached her heart at the sight of the gray eyes looking at her so sadly. She tossed her head, refusing to respond to his unspoken plea, and ran lightly up the steps and through the door into the spacious foyer of her house. Mrs. Ellis, the caretaker, looked rather taken aback at the entrance of her mistress accompanied by a group of strangers.

"My lady, I didn't expect—"

"That's all right, Mrs. Ellis," Eleanor interrupted. "Prepare a bedroom for Mr. Ferret, but the earl will be staying at the Cock and Lantern tonight. Did you prepare my room?" At the housekeeper's nod, Eleanor continued through the hall and up the staircase. "You will excuse me, please. I must have time to recover. Betty, I shall need your services. Mr. Ferret, I'll see you in an hour." With nothing more than a curt nod to her husband, Eleanor disappeared from view.

"Well, m'boy, seems as though you've quite a piece of business to straighten out here. It will take strong measures, I'm thinking." Mr. Ferret turned to Mrs. Ellis. "Do you think you could bring some wine and a few biscuits to the drawing room for us? It's been a hot, dusty ride."

"I think I'd better be going," Geoffrey said somberly. "There's no sense my upsetting Linnet any more than she is." For the first time in his life, the earl felt helpless. He had finally recognized his love for his wife, only to find that she wanted no part of him.

"What? Give up the war without having fought a single battle? Shame on you, my boy!" Mr. Ferret admonished. "You just come along with me, and let's talk this out a while. I don't think you've lost yet."

The two men found their way to the large white-and-gold room where they made themselves comfortable on a pair of sofas. "Now, what you have to keep in mind, son, is that our Linnet has been hurt by your carryings on with that baggage. She has to be assured that you really love her, because you can be sure she loves you. She's also had quite a shock today, being taken captive by that rascal and handled who knows how. She's still just a woman and delicate in her sensibilities, no matter what she says. This whole thing reminds me of a time... Oh thank you, Mrs. Ellis, we'll help ourselves." He interrupted himself to pour the wine. "Now, where was I? Oh, yes, this all reminds me of the time my wife and I had a spat over some silly thing or other. She wouldn't talk to me, wouldn't share my bed, wouldn't let me near her. Had to take her by surprise, I did. So one fine day, when I'd had enough of this nonsense, I waited until we were at dinner. The servants had finished bringing in the food—we were at the desserts I think—and had left the room. I got up, locked the doors, and proceeded to start an unholy loud argument with my dear Jane. I let her call me everything under the sun. She scolded me up and she scolded me down, and when she finally ran out of breath, I grabbed her and kissed her breathless. That ended that fracas, and everything's been fine since. I would suggest you try the same thing. Let Eleanor rip at you until she's got all the venom out of her system, then you take over. I guarantee you won't regret it. Just remember, she loves you. By tomorrow at this time, you'll have forgotten all this unpleasantness."

The elderly man took a last sip of wine and rose to his feet. He took out his pocket watch to check the time. "Well, it's time for me to take my leave. You use my quarters here for the nonce. Freshen yourself and then be here when Eleanor comes down." He held out a hand to the earl. "I'll say good-bye to you, Geoffrey. And good luck. You'll probably need some!"

"I hope your advice works, Adolphus," the earl said warmly. "And I thank you with all my heart. Without your good services, God knows what might have been Eleanor's fate."

"Well, she seemed to have been doing well for herself when we arrived. She'll do. No need for thanks. Have a partiality to the gel myself." With a wave of farewell, the lawyer was on his way.

One hour later, Geoffrey again found himself in the drawing room. He heard Eleanor's voice as she descended the stairs. He placed himself near the door to the room and, as soon as his wife had entered, slammed the door shut and turned the key in the lock.

"What?" She whirled around. "Geoffrey, I thought you had gone. What are you doing here?"

"I've decided to stay, my dear." The sweet velvet of his voice sent a shiver up Eleanor's spine. "How are you feeling after your rigorous afternoon?"

"How do you think I feel? I think it's despicable of you to insinuate yourself into my household like this. I only asked you in because I knew you needed—Where's Mr. Ferret?" Her voice rose with suspicion.

"He had to leave. An urgent message from his wife." Geoffrey moved closer to her. "You look very beautiful tonight, my love."

"Don't call me your love, you...you...rake!" She backed away from him, a curl of desire moving in her belly.

"But you are my love, you know that." He reached out for her, relishing the feel of her soft skin under his hand. "Don't move away from me, my love." His hand covered her breast. "I can feel your heart beat. It pounds like mine does. Feel." He took her fingers and placed them over his chest. "I love you, Eleanor. Don't push me away. I've always loved you, but I was afraid to admit it. Please forgive me. I want you to be my wife, now and forever." His lips touched hers tenderly, gradually increasing their pressure until her mouth opened under his. A delicious languor stole over Eleanor, robbing her of any defense she might have mounted.

Nimble fingers sped over buttons, loosening clothes, each helping the other, anxious now for the closeness attainable only with naked flesh. Tremors of desire hardened, softened, sculpted the passion between them as they sank to the floor, limbs entwined. A breathless sharing of love overcame them as they whispered to each other, urging each other on to ecstasy. Fingers found hidden places of sensitivity, skin brushed skin in an erotic caress as the evanescent emotions reached their peak and two people became one. The shudder of fulfillment shook them, and their voices joined in love's song of completion.

Gradually they returned to earth, their love a contract that they had sealed between them, their life together a pleasure about to unfold.

EPILOGUE

CLOUDS SCUDDED ACROSS the afternoon sky, revealing patches of blue. Two figures walked along the beach, their arms wrapped around each other. The tall man, his hair blowing in the wind, leaned protectively over the woman whose *eau-de-nil* dress peeked out from underneath the windswept cloak. A steep escarpment rose behind them, creating a privacy that enclosed them in their love.

"Are you happy, my love?" the man asked.

"More than I ever hoped to be," his wife answered. "This past year has been heaven. Oh, Geoffrey . . ." She turned to him, raising her arms about his neck as he took her into his powerful embrace. "I have something to tell you."

"What, my sweetheart?" He bent his head, touching her lips with his before she could answer. They stood enjoying each other's caresses for several pleasant moments.

"Dearest love, you take me to paradise when you do that," Eleanor murmured. "But you distract me too much."

Geoffrey moved from his wife's side, still holding her hand but pretending to leave her. "You said you have something to tell me."

"Oh, yes. Do you think nine years is too great a difference between children?" She cast him a sidelong glance.

"Well, I never gave it much...Are you telling me—?"

Eleanor had halted her progress and turned once more into her husband's arms. "Yes, Pip is going to have a brother or sister Christmas next."

"Oh, sweet love, nothing could have pleased me more." Geoffrey hugged her to him and then, in an excess of exuberance, picked her up and whirled her around, shouting his joy.

When at last he came to a stop, dizzy and laughing, he sank to the sand, still holding her close, adoring her face. "I never realized how much I missed not knowing Pip as a babe. But this will make up for that." He studied her large golden eyes, her straight nose, her smiling lips. "How could I have forgotten you? How could I have deprived myself of the pleasure and happiness you give me?"

"My beloved, that's in the past," Eleanor whispered. "We found each other, and we found our happiness. We have the rest of our lives to enjoy that." Her mouth sought his, affirming her words. When she lifted her head again, she gazed deeply into his eyes. "Our love and our children's love will erase any events that might have marred our memories. We have only beautiful times ahead of us, Geoffrey, my dearest one. Let us never remember anything else."

WATCH FOR
6 NEW TITLES EVERY MONTH!

Second Chance at Love

____ 05703-7 **FLAMENCO NIGHTS #1** Susanna Collins
____ 05637-5 **WINTER LOVE SONG #2** Meredith Kingston
____ 05624-3 **THE CHADBOURNE LUCK #3** Lucia Curzon
____ 05777-0 **OUT OF A DREAM #4** Jennifer Rose
____ 05878-5 **GLITTER GIRL #5** Jocelyn Day
____ 05863-7 **AN ARTFUL LADY #6** Sabina Clark
____ 05694-4 **EMERALD BAY #7** Winter Ames
____ 05776-2 **RAPTURE REGAINED #8** Serena Alexander
____ 05801-7 **THE CAUTIOUS HEART #9** Philippa Heywood
____ 05978-1 **PASSION'S FLIGHT #16** Marilyn Mathieu
____ 05847-5 **HEART OF THE GLEN #17** Lily Bradford
____ 05977-3 **BIRD OF PARADISE #18** Winter Ames
____ 05705-3 **DESTINY'S SPELL #19** Susanna Collins
____ 06106-9 **GENTLE TORMENT #20** Johanna Phillips
____ 06059-3 **MAYAN ENCHANTMENT #21** Lila Ford
____ 06301-0 **LED INTO SUNLIGHT #22** Claire Evans
____ 06150-6 **PASSION'S GAMES #24** Meredith Kingston
____ 06160-3 **GIFT OF ORCHIDS #25** Patti Moore
____ 06108-5 **SILKEN CARESSES #26** Samantha Carroll
____ 06318-5 **SAPPHIRE ISLAND #27** Diane Crawford
____ 06335-5 **APHRODITE'S LEGEND #28** Lynn Fairfax
____ 06336-3 **TENDER TRIUMPH #29** Jasmine Craig
____ 06280-4 **AMBER-EYED MAN #30** Johanna Phillips
____ 06249-9 **SUMMER LACE #31** Jenny Nolan
____ 06305-3 **HEARTTHROB #32** Margarett McKean
____ 05626-X **AN ADVERSE ALLIANCE #33** Lucia Curzon
____ 06162-X **LURED INTO DAWN #34** Catherine Mills

____ 05816-5 **DOUBLE DECEPTION #63** Amanda Troy
____ 06675-3 **APOLLO'S DREAM #64** Claire Evans
____ 06680-X **THE ROGUE'S LADY #69** Anne Devon
____ 06687-7 **FORSAKING ALL OTHERS #76** LaVyrle Spencer
____ 06689-3 **SWEETER THAN WINE #78** Jena Hunt
____ 06690-7 **SAVAGE EDEN #79** Diane Crawford
____ 06691-5 **STORMY REUNION #80** Jasmine Craig
____ 06692-3 **THE WAYWARD WIDOW #81** Anne Mayfield
____ 06693-1 **TARNISHED RAINBOW #82** Jocelyn Day
____ 06694-X **STARLIT SEDUCTION #83** Anne Reed
____ 06695-8 **LOVER IN BLUE #84** Aimée Duvall
____ 06696-6 **THE FAMILIAR TOUCH #85** Lynn Lawrence
____ 06697-4 **TWILIGHT EMBRACE #86** Jennifer Rose
____ 06698-2 **QUEEN OF HEARTS #87** Lucia Curzon
____ 06850-0 **PASSION'S SONG #88** Johanna Phillips
____ 06851-9 **A MAN'S PERSUASION #89** Katherine Granger
____ 06852-7 **FORBIDDEN RAPTURE #90** Kate Nevins
____ 06853-5 **THIS WILD HEART #91** Margarett McKean
____ 06854-3 **SPLENDID SAVAGE #92** Zandra Colt
____ 06855-1 **THE EARL'S FANCY #93** Charlotte Hines
____ 06858-6 **BREATHLESS DAWN #94** Susanna Collins
____ 06859-4 **SWEET SURRENDER #95** Diana Mars
____ 06860-8 **GUARDED MOMENTS #96** Lynn Fairfax
____ 06861-6 **ECSTASY RECLAIMED #97** Brandy LaRue
____ 06862-4 **THE WIND'S EMBRACE #98** Melinda Harris
____ 06863-2 **THE FORGOTTEN BRIDE #99** Lillian Marsh

All of the above titles are $1.75 per copy

Available at your local bookstore or return this form to:

SECOND CHANCE AT LOVE
Book Mailing Service, P.O. Box 690, Rockville Cntr., NY 11570

Please send me the titles checked above. I enclose _____ .
Include 75¢ for postage and handling if one book is ordered; 50¢ per book for
two to five. If six or more are ordered, postage is free. California, Illinois, New
York and Tennessee residents please add sales tax.

NAME _____

ADDRESS _____

CITY_____ STATE/ZIP_____

Allow six weeks for delivery.   **SK-41**

WHAT READERS SAY ABOUT
SECOND CHANCE AT LOVE BOOKS

"Your books are the greatest!"
—*M. N., Carteret, New Jersey**

"I have been reading romance novels for quite some time, but the SECOND CHANCE AT LOVE books are the most enjoyable."
—*P. R., Vicksburg, Mississippi**

"I enjoy SECOND CHANCE [AT LOVE] more than any books that I have read and I do read a lot."
—*J. R., Gretna, Louisiana**

"For years I've had my subscription in to Harlequin. Currently there is a series called Circle of Love, but you have them all beat."
—*C. B., Chicago, Illinois**

"I really think your books are exceptional . . . I read Harlequin and Silhouette and although I still like them, I'll buy your books over theirs. SECOND CHANCE [AT LOVE] is more interesting and holds your attention and imagination with a better story line . . ."
—*J. W., Flagstaff, Arizona**

"I've read many romances, but yours take the 'cake'!"
—*D. H., Bloomsburg, Pennsylvania**

"Have waited ten years for *good* romance books. Now I have them."
—*M. P., Jacksonville, Florida**

*Names and addresses available upon request